Purposeful Life
Strategies to living life with purpose

Lame Lesego Rakgantswana

Ukiyoto Publishing

All global publishing rights are held by

Ukiyoto Publishing

Published in 2024

Content Copyright © Lame Lesego Rakgantswana

ISBN 9789367959251

All rights reserved.
No part of this publication may be reproduced, transmitted, or stored in a retrieval system, in any form by any means, electronic, mechanical, photocopying, recording or otherwise, without the prior permission of the publisher.

The moral rights of the author have been asserted.

This is a work of fiction. Names, characters, businesses, places, events, locales, and incidents are either the products of the author's imagination or used in a fictitious manner. Any resemblance to actual persons, living or dead, or actual events is purely coincidental.

This book is sold subject to the condition that it shall not by way of trade or otherwise, be lent, resold, hired out or otherwise circulated, without the publisher's prior consent, in any form of binding or cover other than that in which it is published.

www.ukiyoto.com

Dedication

This book is dedicated to all those who want to live life with purpose and work on accomplishing their goals and all the wonderful people who strive for good impact, changing the world for better. Gratitude and love will forever be with you.

Contents

Dedication	5
Introduction	1
Chapter 1	5
Begin a new era	6
Power of inner dialogue	7
Vision with execution	9
Chapter 2	11
Your unique power	12
The greatest advocate	13
Be genuine and authentic	15
Chapter 3	17
Be the person you want	18
Remove distractions	21
Ignore opinion, focus on purpose	23
Chapter 4	25
Losing toxic people	26
Realize real lies	28
Truly caring people	30
Chapter 5	32
Your natural state	33
Live humbled life	35
Choices during anger	38
Chapter 6	40
True strength and beauty	41
You are stronger	43
Speak your heart	45

Chapter 7 — 46

Trust your path — 47
Answer within — 49
Unplug unnecessary things — 51

Chapter 8 — 54

Live in the present — 55
Stay in the moment — 57
Be like trees — 59

Chapter 9 — 61

Maintain your aura — 62
Change can be painful — 64
Embrace differences — 66

Chapter 10 — 68

Minds are magnets — 69
Earn with your mind — 71
Discuss ideas — 73

Chapter 11 — 75

Think differently — 76
Shifting mindset — 78
Choose to evolve — 80

Chapter 12 — 82

Limitless possibilities — 83
Embrace discomfort — 85
Embracing the truth — 87

Chapter 13 — 89

Stay away from negativity — 90
We cannot force people — 93
Choosing to leave — 95

Chapter 14 — 97

No one is perfect — 98

Pursue your future — 100
Always be humble — 102

Chapter 15 — 104

Don't attach yourself — 105
Stop seeking for love — 107
You are loved — 109

Chapter 16 — 111

Live in peace — 112
Save your energy — 114
Don't absorb, just observe — 116

Chapter 17 — 118

Lead by example — 119
Be optimistic and believer — 121
People come and go — 123

Chapter 18 — 125

Keep the brain engaged — 126
Value your own needs — 127
Don't wait for the right moment — 129

Chapter 19 — 132

Embrace silence and be comfortable — 133
Free yourself from criticism — 135
Create space for clarity — 137

Chapter 20 — 139

Focus on improving — 140
A person is unknown — 142
Pushing someone to improve — 144

Chapter 21 — 146

Be good to yourself — 147
Try after failing — 149
Choose your company wisely — 150

Chapter 22 — 152

Navigate relationships and connections — 153
Healers confront pain — 155
Respecting your journey — 157

Chapter 23 — 159

Integrity and alignment — 160
Avoid comparison with others — 162
Don't seek revenge — 164

Chapter 24 — 165

Understanding constructive criticism — 166
Be harder to manipulate — 168
Accepting people — 170

Chapter 25 — 172

Reflection of thoughts — 173
Let go of anger — 175
Live with harmony — 177

Chapter 26 — 179

Don't tolerate disrespect — 180
Be a well-rounded person — 183
Stand for reason — 186

Chapter 27 — 187

Recognise intentions — 188
Mutual Relationships — 190
Choose calm over conflict — 193

Chapter 28 — 195

Be kind — 196
Your attention is an asset — 198
Self-betrayal — 200

Chapter 29 — 202

Find happiness — 203

Stop being overwhelmed 205
Choose energy givers 208

Chapter 30 210

Trust in the journey 211
Accepting criticism and compliments 213
Reality of life 216

Chapter 31 218

True clarity 219
Emotions are visitors 220
Avoid arguments 223

Chapter 32 225

People change 226
Take time to heal 228
Acknowledge suffering 230

Chapter 33 232

Accountability 233
Foster curiosity 236
Live with integrity 238

Chapter 34 240

Strengthen your faith 241
Embrace small things 243
Earth's time is limited 245

Chapter 35 247

Willing to let go 248
Right people appreciate 251
Stronger than pain 253

Chapter 36 255

Believe in yourself 256
Excuses make tomorrow harder 258
Empowering thoughts 261

Chapter 37 — 264

- Embrace hardships — 265
- Lifted from dark moments — 267
- Never chase and expect — 269

Chapter 38 — 271

- Master your inner world — 272
- Anger is self-punishment — 274
- Don't be easily offended — 276

Chapter 39 — 278

- God is in control — 279
- Stop worrying — 281
- Stop doubting yourself — 283

Chapter 40 — 285

- Break free from expectations — 286
- Enjoy the moment — 288
- Love yourself — 290

About the Author — *292*

Introduction

This book is about pursuing your purpose and living life with purpose.

Chapter 1 is about beginning a new era in life and recognizing the power of inner dialogue. This Chapter is also about having a vision and taking action to accomplish the vision.

Chapter 2 is about embracing your unique power, understanding that you are your own greatest advocate, encourages you to be genuine and authentic.

Chapter 3 is about being the person you want to be, removing distractions and ignoring opinion to focus on your purpose.

Chapter 4 is about losing toxic people in your life, realizing real lies that are told in order to try to manipulate you and understanding that there are truly caring people in your life,

Chapter 5 is about embracing your natural state, living humbled life and making wise choices during anger.

Chapter 6 is about recognizing true strength and beauty, recognizing that you are stronger and speaking your heart.

Chapter 7 is about trusting your path in life, recognizing that the answer to your problems comes from within yourself and to unplug unnecessary things.

Chapter 8 is about living in the present, staying in the moment and be like trees when it loses a leaf during seasons, it grows new a leaf.

Chapter 9 is about maintain your aura, understanding that change can be painful and embracing differences.

Chapter 10 is about acknowledging that our mind are magnets, they attract what we thick about, to use the brain by earning with your mind and to discuss ideas to generate business plans.

Chapter 11 is about understanding that different people think differently, to shift the mindset to an optimistic perspective and choose to evolve with changing aspects of life.

Chapter 12 is about recognizing limitless possibilities, embracing discomfort and embracing the truth in life.

Chapter 13 is about staying away from negativity, how we cannot force people to be our life or do what we want or choose us and finally chapter 13 is about how someone can choose to leave the relationship or negativity.

Chapter 14 is about acknowledging that no one is perfect, pursuing your future and always be humble in life.

Chapter 15 is about how someone should not attach themself to other people too much that they depend on them, to stop seeking for love and understanding that you are loved.

Chapter 16 is about living life with peace and saving your energy. The chapter is also about not absorbing things happening in life and just to observe things happening in life.

Chapter 17 is also about leading by example, being optimistic and being a believer in possibilities. This chapter is also about understanding that people come and go.

Chapter 18 is about keeping the brain engaged, valuing your own needs, taking action and not waiting for the right moment in life.

Chapter 19 is about embracing silence and being comfortable, freeing yourself from criticism and creating space for clarity.

Chapter 20 is about focusing on improving, understanding that a person can be unknown and how pushing someone to improve themselves helps them achieve their goals.

Chapter 21 is about being good to yourself, trying after failing and choosing your company wisely.

Chapter 22 is about navigating relationships and connections, understanding healers confront pain and respecting your journey.

Chapter 23 is about integrity and alignment, avoiding comparison with others and to never seek revenge.

Chapter 24 is about understanding constructive criticism, being harder to manipulate and accepting people with their characters.

Chapter 25 is about reflecting on your thoughts, letting go of anger and living with harmony.

Chapter 26 is about not tolerating disrespect, being a well-rounded person and standing firm for reason.

Chapter 27 is about recognizing intentions, maintaining healthy mutual relationships and choosing to remain calm over conflict.

Chapter 28 is about being kind, understanding that your attention is an asset. This chapter is also about understanding self-betrayal in life.

Chapter 29 is about finding happiness, stop being overwhelmed and choosing energy givers in life.

Chapter 30 is about trusting your journey, accepting reality of life, criticism and compliments in life.

Chapter 31 is about having true clarity, understanding that emotions are visitors and avoiding arguments

Chapter 32 is about understanding that people change, taking time to heal and acknowledge suffering in life.

Chapter 33 is being accountable, fostering curiosity and living life with integrity.

Chapter 34 is about strengthen your faith, embracing small things and understanding that earth's time is limited.

Chapter 35 is about willing to let go, cherishing that the right people will appreciate you and staying stronger than pain.

Chapter 36 is about believing in yourself, understanding that excuses make tomorrow harder and embracing empowering thoughts.

Chapter 37 is about embracing hardships, being lifted from dark moments, not having expectations and never chasing other people.

Chapter 38 is about mastering your inner world, understanding that anger is self-punishment and not to get easily offended.

Chapter 39 is about believing that God is in control of everything, to stop worrying and stop doubting yourself.

Chapter 40 is about breaking free from expectations, enjoying the moment and loving yourself.

Chapter 1

Begin a new era

Every fall is the beginning of a new era. When you're in the midst of a struggle, it's easy to feel like everything is falling apart, like you've lost control, and nothing will ever be the same. But perhaps that's the point, things are not meant to be the same. Every time life knocks you down, it's giving you an opportunity to rise, not as the person you were, but as someone stronger, wiser, and more resilient.

Falling, as painful as it is, creates space for growth. When you're forced to confront challenges, you also confront the parts of yourself that may need to change. Struggles push you to shed old habits, outdated beliefs, and limitations that no longer serve you. What emerges from those difficult times is a new version of you, one that has been forged through the fire of adversity. The person who stands up after the fall is not the same person who stumbled.

Think back to the hardest moments in your life. Even in the pain, confusion, and frustration, something within you shifted. You grew. You learned. Those moments of hardship didn't just knock you down, they reshaped you into someone more capable of navigating life's challenges. Every fall teaches you something about yourself, something you couldn't have learned if everything had stayed easy.

This isn't to say that falling is easy or enjoyable. It's hard, and it hurts. But each time you rise again, you do so with a new perspective and renewed strength. Every fall is an invitation to step into a new chapter, to let go of the person you were, and to become someone new.

So when you find yourself falling, remember: this is the start of something new. The struggle is not your end, it's your transformation. Rise, and embrace the person you're becoming.

Power of inner dialogue

Your inner dialogue is a powerful force. Many of us, often unconsciously, speak to ourselves in ways that limit our potential. Whether it's self-doubt, fear of failure, or harsh self-criticism, these thoughts act as barriers to personal development. But here's the important truth: you have the power to rewrite those thoughts. By consciously choosing to speak to yourself with kindness and encouragement, you open the door to growth. When you start replacing "I can not" with "I'm learning" or "I always fail" with "I'm getting stronger with each try," your mindset shifts. This shift creates a foundation for confidence and resilience, allowing you to embrace challenges and opportunities with a sense of purpose and self-belief.

Beyond your inner dialogue, the people you surround yourself with are equally influential. Those closest to you have the power to either uplift you or hold you back. Choose to invest your energy in relationships that encourage your growth. Surround yourself with individuals who challenge you in healthy ways, inspire you to be your best, and support you through your journey. These are the people who remind you of your potential, even when you may not see it in yourself.

In addition to the company you keep, be mindful of what you consume daily, whether through media, books, or conversations. What you feed your mind and spirit directly impacts your perspective on life. Fill your world with things that inspire creativity, teach you something new, or motivate you to pursue your goals. Choose influences that contribute to your growth, that push you to think bigger, and that remind you of the endless possibilities ahead.

Remember, growth requires a fertile environment. You can't grow in a toxic, negative space. Just as plants need sunlight and water to thrive, your mind needs positivity, encouragement, and hope to flourish. Pay attention to the thoughts, influences, and environments that allow you to grow. Be deliberate about what you let in, and you'll begin to see how much power you have over your own growth and success.

Life is a constant process of growth, and it's up to you to curate the thoughts, influences, and environments that help you evolve. By focusing on what helps you flourish, you are setting the stage for continuous personal development and a life aligned with your potential. Growth is a choice, and every day offers the chance to nurture that potential within you.

Vision with execution

Vision without execution is just hallucination. It's easy to dream, to have grand ideas and ambitions swirling in your mind. We all have visions of who we want to become, what we want to achieve, and how we'd like our lives to unfold. But without action, those visions remain nothing more than fleeting thoughts. Simply thinking about doing something doesn't bring it into existence it's the execution, the hard work, and the follow-through that turn dreams into reality.

How many times have you thought about a project, a goal, or a change you wanted to make in your life, only to watch it fade away because no real steps were taken? This happens to all of us. We get caught up in the excitement of the idea itself, but when it comes time to actually do the work, we hesitate, delay, or avoid it entirely. The dream stays in our minds, unrealized, and eventually disappears.

This is where the difference between dreaming and doing becomes clear. Vision is important it's the spark that ignites creativity and purpose. But without execution, it's empty. No matter how great your ideas are, they remain intangible unless you take action. Execution is the bridge between where you are and where you want to be.

You can plan and visualize all you want, but real progress comes from putting in the effort, taking consistent steps, and following through on your ideas. Think of vision as the destination, but execution is the road that leads you there. Without the road, you never move forward. The vision remains distant, and the gap between your current life and the one you imagine stays just as wide.

Many people fall into the trap of overthinking. They spend hours imagining the perfect scenario, envisioning how their life will change, but they don't take the first step. It's not that they lack the ability to execute; it's that they get stuck in the comfort of the vision itself. They become so used to the dream that they forget it requires effort to bring it into the real world.

Action doesn't have to be big or perfect; it just has to happen. Small, consistent steps are often the most effective way to turn a vision into reality. When you start taking action, even in small ways, you build momentum. You begin to realize that the dream you held in your mind can actually exist in the physical world. The more you do, the clearer the path becomes, and the closer you get to achieving your vision.

But remember, execution isn't always easy. It requires discipline, focus, and persistence. You'll face obstacles, setbacks, and moments of doubt. There will be times when the work feels overwhelming, and you'll want to retreat back into the comfort of just thinking about the goal instead of doing the work. But that's where true progress happens when you push through the discomfort and keep moving forward.

If you want to see your vision come to life, you have to be willing to take action, to step out of your mind and into the real world. The ideas you have are valuable, but they only hold meaning when paired with the effort to make them a reality. Thinking about success doesn't create success. Working toward success does.

So, next time you catch yourself daydreaming about what you want, ask yourself: "What's the first step I can take right now?" Then, take it. Don't wait for the perfect moment or ideal circumstances. Start where you are, with what you have, and build from there. The execution may not always be smooth or easy, but it's what transforms vision into reality.

Vision alone is beautiful, but without action, it's just a hallucination. Don't let your dreams stay stuck in your mind bring them into the world through execution.

Chapter 2

Your unique power

The world needs you to be who you were made to be. Each of us carries a unique power within, but too often, we neglect our true essence. We get caught up in expectations, fear, or comparison, and in doing so, we forget the incredible potential that lies dormant inside us. But the truth remains: only you can unlock the gifts, talents, and purpose that are uniquely yours. No one else in this world can do that for you.

It's easy to look outside of ourselves for answers, validation, or direction, but the reality is, everything you need is already within you. Others can offer guidance and support, but the power to unlock your potential is something only you can access. You alone hold the key to becoming the person you were made to be, and the world is waiting for you to step into that truth.

When we neglect our true essence, we not only short change ourselves but also deprive the world of the impact we are meant to make. You were made for something special, your unique combination of strengths, experiences, and perspective is needed. The moment you decide to honour your true self and embrace your potential, everything changes. The world needs your authentic self, not the version of you shaped by doubt or fear.

Take a step forward. Reconnect with who you truly are, trust in your unique power, and believe in the potential that only you can unlock. The world is waiting for you to rise into your fullest expression, and you are more than capable of making it happen.

The greatest advocate

You are the only person who can truly give yourself what you want. It may seem like a simple statement, but its depth holds a transformative truth. While the world is filled with well-meaning advice, guidance from others, and external opinions, no one else knows what you need as deeply as you do. You are the only one who carries the full picture of your desires, dreams, and longings. Others can offer suggestions or support, but at the core, you are the architect of your own fulfilment. Only you know what will truly make you feel alive, at peace, and whole.

Think about how often we look to others to tell us what we want, whether it's family, friends, or society at large. We are conditioned from a young age to seek validation and approval from outside sources, often leading us to doubt our own instincts and desires. We are told what is "acceptable" to want, what success looks like, or what happiness should feel like. But in doing so, we lose touch with our inner voice, the one that quietly guides us toward our true desires. This voice knows the kind of life you want to live, the passions that make you feel most alive, and the relationships that will bring you joy and fulfilment. Yet, we often silence it, seeking external validation instead.

The truth is, no one else can define your path for you. No one else can know the deepest yearnings of your heart. Even those closest to you, those who love you the most, can only offer perspectives based on their own experiences and perceptions. They don't carry your exact dreams, struggles, or aspirations. They don't feel the inner pull you do when you think about what truly excites you or what brings you peace. That inner knowledge is yours alone, and it is a gift.

We often find ourselves searching outside for what only we can provide. We look for someone to tell us we are on the right path, that we are making the right choices, or that our dreams are worth pursuing. But the only person who can give you that affirmation is you. You are the one who knows what feels right and what doesn't, what resonates with your soul and what leaves you feeling empty. No one else can see the complete picture of your inner world as clearly as you can.

This realization comes with great power. Once you recognize that you are the only one who can give yourself what you truly want, you reclaim ownership of your life. You stop waiting for external approval or permission to go after your dreams. You stop looking to others to fulfil the gaps in your happiness or sense of purpose. You begin to trust yourself and your ability to create the life you desire, on your terms.

This doesn't mean that others can't contribute to your happiness. They can, and they do. Relationships, connections, and support from others are essential parts of a meaningful life. However, the core of your fulfilment must come from within. Others can't give you what only you can. They can't fill a void that stems from ignoring your true desires. Only you know the direction your life should take, and only you can decide to follow it.

Trusting yourself is not always easy. We are often taught to second-guess our instincts, to follow the paths laid out by others, or to adhere to societal norms. But the more you practice listening to your inner voice, the clearer it will become. The more you honour your true desires, the more aligned your life will feel. You'll begin to recognize that you don't need others to validate your choices because you've found that certainty within yourself.

The journey to giving yourself what you truly want starts with self-awareness. Take the time to get quiet, to listen, and to ask yourself what it is you truly desire. Strip away the expectations of others and focus on what brings you joy, peace, and fulfilment. Once you do, you'll realize that the power to create the life you want has been within you all along.

In the end, you are your own greatest advocate, your own best guide, and the only person who can truly give yourself what you need. Listen to that voice within, it knows the way. The more you trust it, the more you will find yourself living a life that is authentically yours, filled with what you truly want and deserve.

Be genuine and authentic

A person who transcends friendship and embodies the essence of a truly good human understands the deeper meaning of connection. They aren't simply present as a friend in the traditional sense, but rather, they become a source of unwavering support, compassion, and understanding for those around them. Their ability to hold space for another person's vulnerabilities, struggles, and fears without judgment or agenda reflects a profound grasp of what it means to be human.

This individual doesn't just listen to others; they offer something far more valuable protection and freedom. When someone opens up to them, they don't try to fix or minimize the problem. Instead, they provide a safe haven where the person feels free to express their emotions and thoughts without fear of being judged or dismissed. This kind of freedom allows people to reveal their true selves, unburdened by the need to hide or edit their feelings. In offering this, the individual grants the other person an invaluable gift: the permission to be fully human.

But what truly distinguishes this person is their understanding of confidentiality and trust. They realize that when someone shares their deepest fears or most painful struggles, it's a sacred act of trust. This person never betrays that trust by divulging private matters or using them against the person in moments of vulnerability. They honour the confidentiality of what's shared, ensuring that those who come to them can do so without hesitation, knowing their struggles are safe.

The way this person interacts with others transcends the boundaries of typical friendship because they operate from a place of selflessness. They don't support others for personal gain or recognition; they do it because they genuinely care about the well-being of others. Their empathy runs so deep that they can truly understand the weight of another person's pain and offer a sense of comfort and solace without making the situation about themselves.

This is what sets them apart an ability to offer care without seeking to control or fix, simply to be there and provide strength through presence.

By embodying these qualities, they exemplify what it means to be a good human at its core. They recognize that being human is about more than just superficial interactions it's about being a source of refuge, offering kindness and understanding to those who need it most. Their actions demonstrate that they grasp the true essence of human connection: that people need not only companionship but someone they can trust with their innermost struggles.

In transcending the typical dynamics of friendship, this person shows us what it means to be truly good. They remind us that kindness, compassion, and confidentiality are at the heart of all meaningful relationships. More than anything, they exemplify that a good human is someone who understands and respects the fragility of others and chooses to uplift, protect, and honour them in every way possible. This level of care transcends friendship; it is the essence of genuine humanity.

Chapter 3

Be the person you want

The key to becoming the person you want to be is not just thinking about who they are, but actively embodying that version of yourself every day. It's easy to dream about who you want to be in the future whether it's someone more confident, successful, compassionate, or disciplined but to truly evolve into that person, you must take consistent action now. This process begins with a shift in mindset: asking yourself, "What would the person I want to be do in this situation?"

Thinking about your future self in this way encourages you to make choices that align with your ideal version. Instead of being held back by your current habits, limitations, or self-doubt, you begin to act as if you're already the person you want to become. This shift is incredibly powerful because it takes you out of a reactive mindset one that is influenced by your present circumstances and moves you into a proactive state of being, where you consciously choose your responses, behaviours, and actions based on the person you aspire to be.

For example, if your goal is to become more confident, think about how a confident person would handle a situation where they might typically feel insecure. How would they walk into a room? How would they approach conversations, challenges, or opportunities? Once you have a clear picture, the next step is to embody that confidence, even if it feels uncomfortable at first. You don't have to wait for confidence to magically appear. By acting confidently, you gradually develop the actual feeling of confidence. Your actions create your reality.

This principle applies to every area of life. If you aspire to be more disciplined, ask yourself what a disciplined person's daily routine would look like. What would they prioritize? How would they stay focused on their goals? Then, implement those habits into your own life, even if it's challenging in the beginning. The more you act in line with the discipline you seek, the more you train yourself to adopt it as a part of who you are.

The key to this transformation is consistency. One day of acting like the person you want to be won't lead to lasting change. But when you commit to thinking and acting like that person every day, your behaviours and mindset begin to align with your future self. Over time, the habits and qualities you aspire to develop become ingrained, and you'll realize that you're no longer just pretending you've truly become the person you wanted to be.

This process is about taking ownership of your evolution. Too often, we wait for external circumstances to change before we feel ready to step into a new version of ourselves. We think, "Once I have more experience, more success, or more confidence, then I'll be ready." But the truth is, waiting keeps you stuck. You have the power to begin that transformation today, simply by choosing to act like the person you want to be.

It's also important to remember that this transformation isn't about perfection. You don't have to get it right all the time. Some days, it will be easier to embody the traits of your future self, while other days you might fall back into old patterns. What matters is your commitment to returning to that mindset, no matter how many times you stray. Every step you take toward acting like the person you want to be, no matter how small, brings you closer to your goal.

Additionally, embodying your future self doesn't just benefit you it positively impacts the people around you. When you act as the best version of yourself, you influence others by setting an example of growth, resilience, and authenticity. Your energy and actions inspire those around you to reflect on their own paths and perhaps even take steps toward becoming their best selves as well.

In the end, becoming the person you want to be isn't something that happens by chance or in the distant future. It's something you create every day by making deliberate choices. By thinking about how your ideal self would act and then embodying those traits in your daily life, you are actively shaping your future. You don't have to wait for circumstances to be perfect or for external validation. You already have the power to be that person it starts with how you choose to think, behave, and show up today.

Remove distractions

You have to remove some things to remain with the right thing. Life is much like tending to a garden, sometimes, for new growth to flourish, you need to clear away the old, the unnecessary, and the distractions. We often carry so much with us, past habits, outdated beliefs, toxic relationships, or even a lifestyle that no longer serves who we are becoming. To grow, transform, and welcome new things into your life, you must first make space. And that space only comes when you let go of what no longer serves you.

Transformation and personal growth demand change. But change is uncomfortable because it often requires us to leave behind what feels familiar, even when that familiarity isn't helping us. It's natural to cling to old patterns, people, or situations that we've outgrown because they give us a sense of security. But if you want to evolve, you must learn to release what is holding you back. When you hold onto everything, there's no room left for anything new to enter your life.

Consider the many distractions that keep you from growing into your true potential. Distractions can take many forms, negative relationships that drain your energy, habits that waste your time, or mindsets that keep you stuck in the past. These distractions act like clutter in your mind and heart, blocking your ability to focus on what truly matters. They pull you in different directions, diluting your energy and preventing you from fully committing to the things that will propel you forward.

Personal growth requires clarity and focus. When you are constantly surrounded by distractions, you lose sight of your goals, your purpose and your potential. It's like trying to move forward with too many weights tied to your ankles, you're dragging things behind you that are slowing you down. And those weights are often things you no longer need but haven't yet let go of.

But here's the beautiful truth: when you begin to let go, space opens up. And in that space, new opportunities, new relationships, and new perspectives can enter. The process of releasing isn't just about loss, it is about making room for something better. It's about realizing that not everything is meant to stay, and that's okay. When you remove the clutter, you begin to see the path forward more clearly. You discover that the very things you've been holding onto out of comfort or fear are the same things blocking you from the life you truly want.

Transformation happens when you trust the process of letting go. It's an act of faith, believing that by removing the things that no longer serve you, you are inviting something better to take their place. It might feel difficult at first, you may feel a sense of emptiness or uncertainty, but that emptiness is not something to fear. It's space for growth. It's a blank canvas where you can begin to create the life you want, free from the distractions that were holding you back.

The reward for letting go and focusing on the right things is immense. When you remove what's wrong, what's unnecessary, or what no longer aligns with your purpose, you begin to align with the right opportunities, the right people, and the right mindset. You start to grow into the person you were always meant to be. And that is the true reward, becoming the best version of yourself, unhindered by distractions, free from the past, and open to new possibilities.

So, take a moment to reflect: What are the things in your life that you need to let go of? What distractions are pulling you away from your true path? What habits, relationships, or beliefs are preventing you from growing into your full potential? The answers may not be easy, but they are essential for your transformation.

Remember, you have to remove some things to remain with the right thing. It's not about loss, it's about making space for what's meant to come. And when you do, you'll find that the reward on the other side is greater than you ever imagined. It's not just about gaining something new; it's about becoming someone new. Someone stronger, wiser, and more aligned with your true purpose. The reward is your own transformation.

Ignore opinion, focus on purpose

Many of the opinions we hold are not entirely our own. While we often believe our thoughts and beliefs are unique, they are frequently shaped by those around us family, friends, society, and the media. What's striking is how subtly this happens. From childhood, we are influenced by the voices we trust, internalizing their perspectives without even realizing it. Over time, these external ideas begin to blend seamlessly with our thinking, and we start to accept them as our own. However, many of the beliefs we claim as ours are, in fact, reflections of someone else's ideas.

This process occurs subtly. We absorb opinions from the people we admire, societal norms, and even passing remarks from strangers or media figures. It's part of human nature to be shaped by the world we live in. As social creatures, our thoughts are influenced by the conversations, media, and experiences around us. The problem arises when we don't take the time to question whether these opinions actually align with who we are and what we stand for. Without realizing it, we can find ourselves living by others' beliefs, not our own.

Consider how often we accept certain viewpoints without critically examining them. For example, we might adopt political stances or life philosophies because they've been reinforced by our environment, or we may choose a career path based on what others expect of us. Over time, we begin to operate under the assumption that these decisions are truly ours, when in reality, they've been subtly shaped by external influences.

To break this cycle, we need to develop self-awareness and recognize when our opinions are borrowed from others. This doesn't mean external influences are inherently bad; they can provide valuable guidance. However, we must pause and reflect: "Is this belief mine, or have I simply inherited it? "By questioning the origins of our beliefs, we can start to separate the ideas that truly resonate with us from those that don't.

This subtle shaping of our thoughts can make it difficult to recognize that our beliefs are not entirely our own. It's important to ask ourselves: "Why do I believe this? Where did this opinion come from?" Only through reflection can we truly distinguish between what feels authentic and what has been subtly adopted from others. This process allows us to reclaim ownership of our thoughts and beliefs, ensuring that they align with our values.

Exploring different perspectives can also help. By exposing ourselves to diverse viewpoints through reading, conversations, or new experiences we challenge the opinions we've absorbed and open our minds to new possibilities. The more we question and explore, the closer we come to discovering what genuinely resonates with us.

Ultimately, acknowledging that our opinions are subtly shaped by others is the first step toward living authentically. Once we recognize this, we can sift through our thoughts, keeping what aligns with our true selves and letting go of what doesn't. This is how we transition from living according to others' influences to embracing a life that's truly our own.

Chapter 4

Losing toxic people

Losing toxic people is a win, even if it doesn't feel like it at first. Toxic relationships, whether they're with friends, family, or partners, can be difficult to let go of because they often blur the lines between love, loyalty, and manipulation. But it's important to recognize the traits of toxic individuals and understand that removing them from your life is not a loss, it's a gain for your well-being and peace of mind.

Toxic people tend to drain your energy rather than uplift you. One of the most prominent traits of a toxic individual is their ability to make everything about themselves. They thrive on control and manipulation, and they often use guilt, criticism, or emotional blackmail to get what they want. You might notice that every conversation seems to revolve around their needs and problems, with little regard for your feelings or boundaries. They rarely show empathy or offer genuine support, leaving you feeling emotionally exhausted after interactions with them.

Another key trait is constant negativity. Toxic people have a way of bringing down the mood with their pessimism, complaints, and drama. No matter how hard you try to stay positive or find solutions, they always find something wrong. Their negative energy can be contagious, dragging you into a cycle of frustration, anxiety, or doubt. Over time, this wears you down, making it harder to see the joy in your own life.

Toxic individuals also often engage in manipulative behaviours like gas lighting, where they make you question your own reality or emotions. They may downplay your achievements, make you feel guilty for standing up for yourself, or twist situations to make it seem like you're always in the wrong. These tactics can undermine your self-esteem and confidence, causing you to doubt yourself in ways you never did before.

A major sign that it's time to leave is the lack of respect for your boundaries. Toxic people often push your limits, whether it's emotional, physical, or mental. They ignore your requests for space or constantly violate your boundaries in subtle ways, making you feel trapped in a cycle of having to explain or justify your needs. Healthy relationships involve mutual respect for boundaries, but in a toxic dynamic, these lines are often crossed, leaving you feeling disrespected and overwhelmed.

It's essential to recognize these behaviours for what they are: signs that the relationship is harmful and not worth holding onto. Walking away from a toxic person isn't a loss; it's a win for your mental and emotional health. It frees up space in your life for healthier relationships where respect, support, and positivity flow naturally. You deserve to be surrounded by people who uplift you, respect your boundaries, and contribute to your growth, not those who hold you back and wear you down.

Cutting ties with toxic individuals can be difficult, especially if they've been a significant part of your life, but it's necessary for your well-being. Their behaviour won't change unless they decide to confront it themselves, and you are not responsible for fixing them. Choosing to let go is an act of self-care, a decision to prioritize your happiness and peace.

In the end, losing toxic people isn't a setback; it's a major step forward. It's a win for your future, your mental health, and your overall quality of life. Surround yourself with those who bring light, not darkness, and you'll soon realize how much better life can be without the weight of toxic influences.

Realize real lies

Real eyes realize real lies, and people who live authentically cannot be fooled. When you embrace truth and honesty in your own life, you develop a keen awareness of what is genuine and what is not. This awareness sharpens your intuition and helps you recognize when others are being disingenuous or trying to manipulate a situation. People who live authentically have no need for pretence, and because of this, they are naturally resistant to the facades and falsehoods of those who are not living truthfully.

Genuine people have walked the path of self-awareness and vulnerability. They've learned the value of being true to themselves, and through that process, they have honed their ability to spot deception. When you live a life based on honesty, you can sense when someone is hiding behind a mask or putting up a front. This doesn't require effort or suspicion rather, it's a natural result of having lived with openness. Those who are real can easily detect when someone is being fake because they understand what it means to be vulnerable, raw, and authentic.

These individuals cannot be fooled because they are not swayed by superficial appearances or empty words. Authentic people are not impressed by charm, flattery, or manipulation. Instead, they seek deeper connections that are built on honesty and mutual respect. They've learned to look beyond the surface and assess the substance of a person's character. When you live a life where truth is central, you naturally become attuned to spotting dishonesty or pretence in others.

In a world filled with distractions, trends, and social pressures, being able to see through deception is a powerful trait. Real people are grounded in their values, and they don't let outside influences cloud their judgment. They aren't easily manipulated by society's expectations or the pressures to conform. Instead, they stay true to who they are, and that clarity allows them to identify when someone is trying to deceive or mislead them.

For those who live authentically, trying to fool them is a futile effort. They've worked hard to remove dishonesty from their own lives, so they won't tolerate it from others. When you embrace your own truth, you are better equipped to navigate a world that often prioritizes appearances over substance. Authentic people value meaningful connections over shallow interactions, and this mindset makes them resistant to deception.

Real people aren't just good at spotting lies they also understand the deeper motivations behind them. They can see when someone is hiding their true intentions, whether out of insecurity, manipulation, or fear. And because they've been through their own process of self-discovery, they know that truth always reveals itself in the end. They understand that trying to live a life based on deception or manipulation is unsustainable and that the only way to build genuine relationships is through honesty and transparency.

In the end, real people cannot be fooled because they have learned to value what truly matters: honesty, authenticity, and depth. Their real eyes can see beyond the masks others wear, and their commitment to truth allows them to navigate life with clarity and strength. They are unshakable because they have built their lives on a foundation of integrity, and that foundation makes them immune to the falsehoods that often permeate the world around them.

Truly caring people

Only those who truly care about you can hear you when you're quiet. This simple truth speaks to the profound connection that exists between people who genuinely care for each other. In these relationships, it's not just about the words spoken, but the understanding that comes from shared experiences, deep empathy, and mutual respect. These are the connections where silence speaks volumes, and even in the absence of words, you are seen, heard, and valued.

At a fundamental level, relationships built on such understanding are deeply satisfying because they provide a sense of security and belonging that goes beyond surface-level interactions. In a world filled with noise and distractions, having someone who can recognize when something is wrong, even when you say nothing, is a rare and precious gift. It's in these moments that the depth of the relationship reveals itself. They know you well enough to sense your struggles or joys without needing an explanation, and this understanding fosters a bond that feels authentic and fulfilling.

True connection with others offers more than just companionship; it satisfies an essential human need for emotional intimacy and support. These relationships are the foundation of a meaningful life because they create spaces where you can be vulnerable without fear of judgment. When someone can hear you in your silence, it means they've taken the time to understand who you are at your core. They see you beyond your outward expressions and care enough to pay attention to the subtleties of your emotional world.

This type of relationship nurtures both individuals, allowing for personal growth and mutual support. It isn't about grand gestures or constant communication; it's about a quiet, steady presence that reassures you that you are not alone. Knowing someone is attuned to your needs, even when you struggle to express them, builds a level of trust that is hard to find in casual interactions. It's these deeper bonds that make life richer, filling it with moments of genuine care and understanding.

At its heart, the ability to be heard in your silence reflects a relationship where both people feel truly seen. These relationships transcend the superficiality that often accompanies everyday interactions and tap into something more meaningful. They are rooted in compassion, patience, and a willingness to be present for each other, no matter the circumstances.

In a world where so much of our communication happens through words, messages, and digital screens, these quiet, deeply connected relationships stand out. They remind us that true fulfillment comes from being with people who don't need us to constantly explain ourselves because they care enough to understand us on a deeper level.

Ultimately, relationships that reach this fundamental level of care are the most rewarding because they nourish our souls. They provide a kind of satisfaction that can't be found in casual acquaintances or fleeting connections. They remind us that life is not just about being seen, but about being truly understood and supported, even in the quietest of moments.

Chapter 5

Your natural state

Your natural state is one of love. It's who you are at your core, beneath the layers of fear, doubt, and self-judgment. Love is not something you need to earn or chase, it is your essence, the vibration you naturally embody when everything else falls away. To return to this state, to live in alignment with your true self, you must let go of everything that suppresses this love. Fear, shame, limiting beliefs, judgments, and feelings of unworthiness all weigh you down, keeping you disconnected from your natural state.

Fear, especially the fear of survival, often dominates our thoughts. We spend so much energy worrying about the future, our security, and our ability to meet life's demands. But this fear holds you in a constant state of stress, preventing you from living fully in the present, where love exists. To return to your natural state, you have to release the need to control every outcome, trusting that you are capable of navigating whatever life brings. Only then can love replace the fear, opening you to the peace that's been waiting for you all along.

Shame from the past is another block that suppresses your vibration. Many of us carry the weight of past mistakes, regrets, and unresolved emotions, believing that we are somehow less worthy because of them. But shame is a heavy chain that keeps you stuck in a version of yourself that no longer exists. To reach the state of love, you must release the hold that the past has over you. You are not your mistakes. You are not your past. When you let go of the shame, you open yourself to the lightness of love and self-compassion.

Limiting beliefs are like invisible walls that keep you from experiencing your true potential. Whether these beliefs tell you that you're not good enough, not smart enough, or not deserving of happiness, they're all rooted in fear and falsehood. These beliefs are not your truth, they are merely stories you've adopted over time. The moment you recognize them for what they are and choose to let them go, your vibration naturally rises. Love flows freely when you stop limiting yourself.

Judgment, both of yourself and others, is another heavy burden that blocks your natural state. When you judge, you're projecting fear and separation, distancing yourself from love. Judgment comes from a place of insecurity and the need to protect yourself from perceived threats. But love does not judge. Love accepts, understands, and embraces. To reach this state, you must let go of the need to compare, to criticize, and to separate. Let go of harsh self-judgment and the constant evaluation of others, and you will find that love naturally fills the space where judgment once lived.

Feelings of unworthiness are perhaps the deepest obstacle to overcome. Many people carry a quiet, lingering belief that they are not worthy of love, happiness, or success. This belief keeps you from fully accepting the love that already exists within and around you. But you are worthy, just by being you. Your worth is inherent, not something to be earned. Once you let go of this false idea of unworthiness, you reconnect with your natural state of love, which has always been waiting for you.

To return to love is to strip away all that suppresses your natural vibration. It's about releasing the fear of survival, the shame of past mistakes, the limiting beliefs that hold you back, the judgments that separate you, and the feelings of unworthiness that cloud your view. Letting go of these things doesn't mean ignoring them or pretending they don't exist, it means acknowledging them, learning from them, and then releasing their grip on your life.

When you let go, you make space for your natural state of love to emerge. Love is your birth right, your essence. It's what remains when fear, shame, and judgment are released. The more you release what no longer serves you, the more you embody this natural state of love, where peace, joy, and compassion become your everyday experience.

You don't have to "find love" you just have to "remember" it. It's already within you. Let go of everything that suppresses it, and watch as your vibration rises, allowing you to live in the fullness of your natural state: pure, unconditional love.

Live humbled life

Life humbles you. As you grow older, you begin to realize that the things you once chased, the big dreams, the grand achievements, the need to prove yourself, slowly lose their allure. What you thought would bring you fulfilment often feels incomplete. Over time, you come to understand that true happiness doesn't lie in the grand, fleeting moments of life, but in the quiet simplicity of everyday existence. The more life teaches you, the more you begin to treasure the little things, those small, seemingly insignificant moments that, when strung together, create a life filled with meaning and peace.

There comes a point when the hustle of chasing after "success" fades, and in its place, you start to long for the simplicity of life, things like enough sleep, time to yourself, nourishing meals, long walks, and the company of those you love. These things may not seem glamorous or ground-breaking, but they hold a quiet power that can ground you in ways that big achievements cannot.

Alone time becomes sacred. As you grow, you realize that solitude is not something to fear or avoid, but something to embrace. It's in those quiet moments with yourself that you reconnect with who you truly are, away from the noise and expectations of the world. Solitude offers clarity, peace, and space for reflection. The time you spend alone is where you nurture your spirit and recharge, making you better equipped to handle the challenges that life inevitably brings.

You start to prioritize your well-being, understanding that enough sleep is no longer a luxury but a necessity. The energy and vitality you need to enjoy life come from taking care of your body. You stop sacrificing sleep for the sake of productivity because you know that true productivity stems from a well-rested mind. Rest, once seen as something secondary, becomes central to your ability to experience life fully.

Diet and nourishment take on a new meaning, too. It's not about following the latest trends or achieving a specific goal; it's about honouring your body with what it needs to thrive. You begin to see food not just as sustenance but as a source of well-being. Eating well becomes an act of self-love, and you find joy in taking care of yourself in the simplest, most essential ways.

Then, there are the long walks. Something as simple as putting one foot in front of the other, moving through the world slowly and mindfully, becomes a meditative practice. Long walks allow you to connect with nature, to quiet your thoughts, and to appreciate the world around you. They remind you that life doesn't have to move at a breakneck speed, that there is beauty in slowing down, in observing the little things, the rustle of leaves, the feel of the breeze, the warmth of the sun. These small experiences, once overlooked, begin to hold immense value.

Perhaps the greatest simplicity of all is the time you spend with loved ones. As life humbles you, you realize that relationships are the true treasures. The moments spent laughing with friends, talking with family, or simply sitting in comfortable silence with someone you care about become the most meaningful. You stop taking these moments for granted. Time spent with loved ones isn't about doing anything extraordinary, it's about the simple act of being together. In the end, these are the moments that matter most.

As you grow older, life teaches you that chasing after big things, the accolades, the recognition, the material wealth, doesn't bring the lasting contentment you once thought it would. Instead, the little things, the things that seem small but hold so much weight, become the ultimate goal. It's the quiet, steady rhythm of daily life that brings true peace. The joy of waking up rested, eating a nourishing meal, going for a long walk, enjoying time with loved ones, and taking time to simply be with yourself, these become the moments that make life rich and fulfilling.

Life humbles you by showing you that the big things you once thought were the key to happiness pale in comparison to the small, simple joys that are always within reach. The more you embrace these moments, the more you find that they hold the true essence of a life well-lived. It is in the simplicity that you find peace, contentment, and a deep sense of gratitude for all that you have.

Choices during anger

Choices made under anger cannot be undone, but anger itself can be diffused with understanding. When we feel anger, it often stems from frustration, a deep sense of powerlessness and a lack of control over a situation or person. But rather than giving in to this emotional surge and making impulsive decisions, the real antidote is understanding: understanding the situation, understanding ourselves, and, perhaps most importantly, understanding others.

Anger is a reactive emotion. It comes quickly, like a storm, clouding our judgment and pushing us to act in ways we often regret. But if we pause long enough to seek understanding in the moment, the entire landscape of that emotion can shift. Instead of letting the frustration control us, we can step back and ask ourselves, "What's really driving this anger?" More often than not, it's a lack of control, a feeling of being misunderstood, or unmet expectations. When we identify the root cause, we can address the actual problem, rather than letting the anger lead us into more chaos.

When we approach anger with understanding, we realize that most situations aren't as personal as they feel in the moment. The person or circumstance that triggers our frustration likely has its own complexities. Maybe the person we're upset with is going through their own struggles, or perhaps the situation we're facing is beyond anyone's control. By taking the time to understand what's happening beneath the surface, we can find empathy, both for ourselves and others. This doesn't mean justifying harmful behaviour, but it does mean seeing the bigger picture and not letting our immediate emotions take over.

Understanding also helps us shift our perspective. Rather than feeling trapped by the anger, we can ask, "How can I respond in a way that helps rather than harms?" This shift in focus from reacting to responding gives us back control. By choosing understanding, we replace impulsive reactions with thoughtful actions. We begin to approach situations with curiosity rather than rage, and through that, we gain clarity.

In situations where we can't change what's happening, understanding helps us accept it without bitterness. Not every situation can be controlled, and not every person will act in ways we expect. But if we approach life with a mindset of understanding, we are less likely to be caught in the trap of anger. Instead of feeling frustrated over what we can't change, we can shift our energy toward what we can, our response, our mind-set, and our ability to seek solutions.

Ultimately, understanding is a powerful tool for combating anger. It helps us step out of the narrow focus that anger creates and opens us up to a broader perspective. When we seek to understand rather than react, we calm the storm within and regain control over our emotions and actions. Anger may come, but with understanding, we can navigate it without letting it lead us astray. We can choose to act with clarity and compassion, turning moments of frustration into opportunities for growth and connection.

Chapter 6

True strength and beauty

What makes these people special isn't just their outer expressions, but the way they move through life with a certain grace. It's as though they have tapped into a well of inner peace, a profound understanding of themselves and the world around them. This confidence isn't flashy or boastful; it's a quiet, grounded assurance that makes you feel more secure just by being near them. Their energy is calm, like still water, and in their presence, you feel your own anxieties and stresses soften, as though their inner light casts away your shadows.

The most remarkable thing about these individuals is that they ask for nothing in return. Their warmth and presence are not transactional; they don't shine to be noticed or to gain anything from others. It's an effortless radiance born from a place of true self-contentment. They do not seek approval or validation, nor do they measure their worth by what they can receive from the world. Instead, their fulfillment comes from within, and because of this, they can give freely, without expectation.

These people embody a deeper truth: that the most powerful influence we can have on others comes not from what we can take or even achieve, but from what we can give, freely and generously. It is the power of inner peace, of living in harmony with oneself, and of being so full within that you naturally spill over, sharing light with others. Their light doesn't dim others; it empowers them. And it's this absence of need or expectation that makes them so magnetic. When we are around them, we don't feel drained or inadequate, but uplifted, as if their light reminds us of our own.

This kind of inner radiance is not something that can be faked or manufactured. It is the result of self-acceptance, of finding peace with oneself and the world. These are people who have faced their own darkness and come out the other side with a deeper understanding, an unshakable confidence that they are enough just as they are. It's not about perfection; it's about wholeness. And in their presence, you feel inspired to seek that same wholeness within yourself.

They show us that true strength and beauty come not from what we display to the world, but from the quiet, steady light we carry within. They teach us that the greatest gifts we can offer others are not things or accolades but our true, unguarded selves. And in a world that often emphasizes what we can achieve, acquire, or take, these sun-like individuals remind us that the most lasting impact comes from what we give, from the light we share simply because it's who we are.

You are stronger

You are stronger than you realize, and you have more control over your life than you sometimes give yourself credit for. There's a fundamental truth that can be both challenging and empowering to accept: often, it's not the circumstances around you that cause the most pain, it's how you respond to them. You may not always see it clearly, but much of the weight you carry, the stress, the self-doubt, and the worry, comes from within. And the good news? Because it comes from within, you have the power to change it.

You might feel overwhelmed at times, as if life is handing you more than you can handle. But take a step back and reflect on how much of the pain comes from your own thoughts, your interpretations, and your reactions. External circumstances can be tough, and challenges will always exist, but often we prolong our suffering by clinging to fears, worries, and doubts. The truth is, it's not the world outside that holds you back as much as your own internal dialogue.

Think about it: how often do you replay old hurts in your mind, picking at emotional wounds that could otherwise heal? How often do you anticipate future difficulties and let fear of the unknown steal your peace? We all do this, it is human nature to worry and to hold onto painful memories. But when you understand that you are the source of much of your own suffering, you open up the possibility of letting it go. You realize that just as you have the power to cause yourself pain, you also have the power to free yourself from it.

You don't need to carry the weight of the past or the anxieties of the future. You have the ability to shift your focus to the present, to what you can control in this moment. The more you practice this, the lighter you'll feel. Your mind is incredibly powerful, and when you start to use that power to choose thoughts that empower you rather than tear you down, your whole life can change.

This doesn't mean that life will be free of challenges, far from it. But when you approach those challenges with a clear mind and a positive outlook, they become less daunting. You'll begin to see difficulties not as insurmountable obstacles, but as opportunities for growth. You've faced challenges before, and you've overcome them. That same resilience exists within you now, waiting for you to trust it.

What's important to recognize is that you have the ability to stop the cycle of self-inflicted pain. You can choose not to replay the hurtful words that were said to you or the mistakes you've made in the past. You can choose to forgive yourself and others, not because they deserve it, but because you deserve peace. You can decide to stop worrying about the things that haven't even happened yet, knowing that you are capable of handling whatever comes your way.

The more you practice letting go of unnecessary mental burdens, the more you'll begin to notice a shift in your emotional and physical well-being. You'll start to feel lighter, more at ease, and more empowered. You'll realize that you are not at the mercy of your circumstances, and you never were. The true power lies in your ability to control your thoughts and reactions.

It takes courage to confront this truth, that much of your pain is self-inflicted. But it's also incredibly freeing. Once you realize that the chains that bind you are of your own making, you understand that you also hold the key to unlocking them. You are in control of your mind, your responses, and ultimately, your experience of life.

So be kind to yourself. Acknowledge the strength that lies within you, the same strength that has carried you through difficult times in the past. Trust that you have the power to not only endure, but to thrive. Release the old patterns of thinking that no longer serve you, and embrace the truth that you are capable of creating a life filled with peace, joy, and resilience.

You've caused yourself pain before, yes. But now you have the opportunity to choose something different. You have the chance to choose thoughts that heal, actions that uplift, and a mind-set that empowers. In doing so, you will find that the strength to overcome anything has always been within you. It's time to stop standing in your own way and start letting yourself rise.

Speak your heart

Your heart knows your deepest desires and your truest dreams, and yet, it is so often silenced by doubt, fear, or external expectations. However, the heart is meant to be listened to, not hidden away. It holds your most profound truths, and when you allow yourself to follow its lead, you open yourself to a life that aligns with your inner self, full of meaning and fulfillment.

The heart doesn't rationalize or conform to societal standards; it simply knows what you need to feel alive and whole. To speak your heart is to embrace your true self without hesitation, to honour your desires without fear of judgment. Your desires, no matter how unconventional or uncertain, are valid. They are a reflection of who you are, and they are worthy of being pursued.

We often convince ourselves that our dreams are impractical or unattainable, letting the world's opinions drown out our inner voice. But this self-suppression leads only to frustration and a sense of unfulfilled potential. The courage to listen to your heart and even more, to act on what it says, opens the door to a life that is true to who you are, not who you're expected to be.

Your heart speaks the language of truth and poetry. It is fearless in its pursuit of what truly matters to you. To speak from your heart is to claim your right to live authentically, to embrace your desires, and to have the courage to pursue them. In doing so, you'll find not only your path but the fulfilment that comes from living in alignment with your deepest self.

Chapter 7

Trust your path

You could never do anything wrong. No matter which path you choose, no matter what decisions you make, there is no wrong way. Life is not about perfect choices or avoiding mistakes, it is about experiencing, growing, and learning from everything that unfolds along the way. Every turn, every step, is part of a greater story that is unfolding perfectly, even if it doesn't always seem that way.

Sometimes, we carry the weight of decisions, fearing that one wrong choice could set us off course or that a single mistake could prevent us from reaching where we want to be. But the truth is, there is no wrong path. Every experience, every challenge, and every triumph is woven into the fabric of your life's journey. Each moment, even the ones that feel difficult or uncertain, is contributing to the bigger picture of who you are becoming.

Think of life as a vast, intricate story. Just like in any great narrative, there are twists and turns, moments of doubt, and unexpected developments. But even the detours and the so-called "mistakes" serve a purpose. They bring depth, understanding, and wisdom. They lead you to new insights, new opportunities, and new connections that you might not have discovered otherwise. The moments that feel like missteps are often the ones that end up bringing the most growth.

You are always exactly where you are meant to be, and you are always moving toward what is meant for you. Even when you feel lost, you are on the right path. Even when things don't go as planned, they are unfolding in the way they need to. There is no need to fear making the wrong decision, because no matter what you choose, you are still loved, still supported, and still on your way to where you are supposed to be.

The universe, or however you define the greater forces at play, is not sitting in judgment of your choices. It is guiding you, gently nudging you forward, no matter what. Every choice you make leads you to more experiences, more growth, and more understanding of who you truly are. Whether a decision leads to immediate success or takes you down a longer, more winding road, it is all part of your unique story.

And in this story, you are never wrong. You are always learning, always evolving, and always moving forward, even when it feels like you've taken a step back. The pressure to be perfect, to make the "right" choice every time, is an illusion. The truth is, life isn't about being perfect; it's about being human. It's about living fully, embracing every part of the journey, and knowing that no matter what happens, you are loved and worthy, just as you are.

So, let go of the fear of making mistakes. Trust that whatever path you choose will serve you in some way, even if it looks different from what you expected. Know that you can never be off track, because every road you take is leading you somewhere important. And in the end, it's not about where you end up, it's about the experiences you collect, the lessons you learn, and the love you share along the way.

You are part of something much bigger than any single decision or moment. Every chapter of your life, even the ones that seem uncertain or challenging, is unfolding in perfect timing. And through it all, you are loved unconditionally. You don't need to prove yourself or make every choice perfectly to be worthy of that love. It's already yours, always has been, and always will be.

So, trust yourself. Trust the path, even when it feels unclear. And remember, you could never do anything wrong. You are exactly where you're meant to be, and you are loved, no matter what.

Answer within

Your soul already knows the answer. Deep within, beneath the noise of daily life, distractions, and doubts, your soul holds the wisdom you seek. It is constantly guiding you, whispering the truths that will lead you to your most authentic path. The challenge, however, is not in finding the answers, it's in getting quiet enough to hear them and being brave enough to follow them.

In a world that is constantly busy, filled with outside influences and expectations, it's easy to forget that we all have an internal compass. We often look outward for direction, asking others for advice, following trends, or seeking validation. But the answers you're searching for don't live out there they live within you. Your soul, the deepest part of who you are, always knows what is right for you. It knows the direction you should take, the decisions that align with your purpose, and the desires that are truly yours.

To access that wisdom, you need to quiet the noise. This doesn't mean shutting yourself off from the world, but rather creating moments of stillness where you can reconnect with yourself. In those quiet moments, whether through meditation, solitude, or simple reflection, your soul has a chance to speak. The answers may not always come in clear words, but through feelings, instincts, and inner knowing. Trust that the clarity you need is already within you, waiting for you to listen.

The difficulty is not in hearing your soul, it's in having the courage to trust it. Once you quiet the external noise and hear that inner voice, fear often creeps in. You might doubt yourself, question whether following your soul's guidance will lead to the unknown, or worry that the path it suggests won't align with the expectations of others. This is where bravery comes in. It takes courage to listen to your soul and even more courage to follow through on what it tells you.

The soul's wisdom often leads us in directions that feel uncertain or unconventional, but that's because it is guiding you to your unique path, not the path someone else has walked, but one that is entirely your own. Following your soul means trusting yourself above all else, even when the world around you is telling you otherwise. It means honouring what you know deep down to be true, even when it feels uncomfortable or unfamiliar.

When you follow the answers your soul provides, you find yourself moving toward a life that feels more authentic, more aligned with who you truly are. You stop living for others or trying to fit into moulds that were never meant for you. Instead, you start living from a place of truth and purpose. This doesn't mean the path will always be easy, listening to your soul often requires stepping into the unknown. But it is a path that will always lead to greater fulfilment and peace because it is the path you were meant to walk.

So, the next time you find yourself searching for answers, pause. Take a moment to get quiet, to step away from the noise, and listen to that inner voice. Your soul already knows the way. Trust that the wisdom is there, waiting for you to hear it. And when you do, be brave enough to follow it. The path your soul leads you on may not always be the easiest, but it will always be the truest. In that truth, you will find not only the answers you seek but the life you were meant to live.

Unplug unnecessary things

Sometimes the best way to recharge is to unplug unnecessary things. We often find ourselves feeling drained, overwhelmed, or simply out of sync, and the reason is not always about how much we are doing but what we are giving our energy to. The truth is, not everything in your life deserves your attention. Many of the things that we engage with on a daily basis, whether it is negative influences, distractions, or toxic environments are unnecessary. They don't contribute positively to our well-being, and more often than not, they drain us.

Imagine for a moment that your energy is like a battery. Each day, you wake up with a certain amount of charge, and everything you do uses some of that energy. The people you interact with, the thoughts you entertain, the environments you engage in all of these things either recharge or deplete you. If you're constantly plugged into things that take more than they give, whether it's negative relationships, toxic social media, or self-doubt you'll find yourself running on empty before the day even begins.

The key to living a more energized, fulfilled life is to unplug from the unnecessary. Anything that doesn't directly benefit your growth, your happiness, or your peace of mind is unnecessary. Life becomes better when you can identify what no longer serves you and have the courage to let it go. By doing this, you create space for positivity to flourish, and you start to refill your battery with things that actually nourish you.

For example, take a look at your relationships. Are there people in your life who constantly bring negativity, drama, or stress? While it's important to be compassionate and understanding, it's equally important to protect your own energy. If someone's presence in your life consistently brings you down rather than lifts you up, it may be time to unplug from that relationship. Surrounding yourself with positivity people who support you, inspire you, and uplift you creates an environment where you can thrive.

The same applies to your habits. Are there activities or routines that leave you feeling depleted? Maybe it's spending too much time scrolling through social media, or maybe it's holding on to self-criticism that dampens your spirit. Unplugging from these unnecessary habits allows you to focus on actions that recharge you. Engage in activities that bring you joy, peace, or a sense of accomplishment things that contribute to your growth and happiness. Whether it's spending time in nature, reading, practicing mindfulness, or pursuing a passion, these are the things that truly recharge your energy.

Negativity, whether in the form of thoughts, people, or habits, is like a drain on your system. It pulls energy from you, leaving you feeling tired and unfulfilled. But when you unplug from those sources of negativity, you stop giving away your power and start reclaiming it. You begin to notice that when you remove the things that deplete you, you naturally create more space for the things that energize you. Life becomes lighter, more purposeful, and filled with the kind of positivity that fuels you rather than drains you.

Unplugging doesn't mean running away from problems or challenges; it means choosing what is truly necessary for your growth and well-being. It's about learning to discern between what is essential and what is simply noise. When you do this, you start to recharge in ways you didn't even know were possible. You free yourself from the weight of unnecessary baggage and open up to a life that is simpler, more joyful, and more aligned with who you are.

By removing unnecessary things, you make room for more of what truly matters. You focus on the relationships that nurture you, the activities that bring you joy, and the habits that support your growth. Life becomes less about managing distractions and more about cultivating positivity. When you let go of what doesn't serve you, you'll find that your energy naturally increases, and you'll be better equipped to face whatever challenges come your way.

So, the next time you feel drained, ask yourself: What can I unplug from? What in my life is unnecessary and no longer serves me? By unplugging from these things, you'll discover that recharging doesn't always come from adding more, it often comes from letting go. Life becomes better, lighter, and more fulfilling when you clear out the negativity and focus on what truly nourishes your soul.

Chapter 8

Live in the present

The only thing that is guaranteed is this moment. As we go through life, we often find ourselves caught up in thoughts about the past or the future, replaying old memories or worrying about what's to come. But the only time that truly exists is now, in this very moment. The past is gone, and the future is uncertain. What we perceive as "time" is nothing more than memory and anticipation living in our minds. Once we fully understand this, we can unlock a deeper sense of peace and presence.

Think about it: the past is a collection of moments that no longer exist except in our memories. We might revisit them, analyse them, or even relive them in our minds, but we cannot step back into them. No matter how much we wish to change or relive the past, it remains beyond our reach, forever out of our control. All we have left of it are the stories we tell ourselves, the emotions it stirs, and the lessons it offers.

Likewise, the future is nothing more than a projection of our imagination. We anticipate what might happen, we plan for what we hope to achieve, and we worry about what we fear may come. But just like the past, the future does not yet exist. It's a mental construct, an idea in your mind that can change at any moment. You can picture a future filled with hope or anxiety, but until it arrives, it remains nothing but anticipation.

When we focus too much on the past, we often find ourselves stuck in regret or nostalgia, longing for something that's already gone. When we focus too much on the future, we experience anxiety or stress, constantly striving toward something that hasn't happened yet. Both take us away from the only time that is real: right now.

Now is the only time in which we can act, make choices, and experience life. In this moment, you are breathing, your heart is beating, and you are alive. This moment holds everything, your thoughts, emotions, and the world around you. When you fully embrace the present, you find that it's the only place where peace, contentment, and clarity exist. There is no fear of what has been or anxiety about what will be. There is just "now".

Understanding that the present is all we ever have allows us to stop chasing what's out of reach and appreciate what is right in front of us. This realization opens a door to mindfulness, where we can engage fully with each moment, experiencing life as it unfolds rather than through the lens of past regrets or future worries. When we do this, we free ourselves from the constant tension of time and discover a deeper connection to ourselves and the world.

The past and future are simply ideas, living in your mind. They are constructs that only exist when you allow your thoughts to drift there. But the present moment is where your life is happening. It is here, now, and it is the only reality you can truly experience. By bringing your attention to the now, you allow yourself to fully live, to make the most of every breath and every experience.

Let go of the need to control what has already passed or what is yet to come. The only thing that is guaranteed is this moment, right now. And when you focus on the present, you realize that life is not something waiting for you in the future or lost in the past. It is happening in the present, always. This is where peace lies, where true joy can be found, and where you can experience the fullness of life.

The past is a memory. The future is anticipation. But the present? The present is life itself. Embrace it fully, for it is the only time that truly exists.

Stay in the moment

Understanding time as an illusion helps you stay in the moment because it changes how you view the past and the future. When we think of time as a straight line, we often get stuck dwelling on what's already happened or worrying about what's yet to come. This can distract us from what's happening right now. But when you realize that the past, present, and future might all exist at once, it shifts your focus. Instead of stressing about things you can't change or events that haven't happened, you start to see that the only thing you really have control over is the present moment.

If everything is connected and happening simultaneously, it means that the choices and actions you make in this very moment are incredibly important. This moment isn't just a stepping stone to the future; it is part of a bigger picture that already exists. By staying in the present, you're participating in this larger reality and affecting it in ways you might not even see yet.

When you adopt this perspective, it becomes easier to let go of the constant anxiety about what's coming or regret over what's already passed. You start to understand that worrying about the future doesn't change it, and holding onto the past doesn't alter what's already happened. The only thing that truly matters is what you do right now, in this moment.

By focusing on the present, you can live more mindfully, paying attention to what's happening around you and within you. You're not wasting energy thinking about things beyond your control. This helps you make better decisions, enjoy your experiences more fully, and feel more connected to your life as it unfolds.

This concept encourages you to live with intention, knowing that every action in the present moment ripples outward into the future, which is already part of the larger whole. Instead of rushing to get to the next phase of life or being stuck in past regrets, you can simply be where you are, knowing that this moment is both enough and essential.

Staying in the moment becomes a powerful way to live, because you're no longer distracted by time as we traditionally understand it. You're free to focus on what's right in front of you, whether it's the people you're with, the tasks you're doing, or the feelings you're experiencing. Living this way creates a sense of peace, purpose, and presence that deepens your connection to yourself and the world around you.

Be like trees

Like trees, you're going to bloom again too! Just as the earth moves through seasons, so do we. Life has its cycles times of growth, times of stillness, and times when things fall away. But just as spring always follows winter, your time to bloom will come again. It's important to remember that the challenges you face now, the quiet moments where it feels like nothing is happening, are just part of the natural rhythm of life.

Trees don't bloom year-round. They shed their leaves, stand bare through the cold, and weather storms. But no matter how harsh the winter, they always bloom again when the season is right. You are no different. Life might feel difficult right now, like you're in your own personal winter, but this season won't last forever. Just as the trees use winter as a time to rest and prepare for growth, this time in your life is preparing you for something new, something better.

It's easy to feel discouraged when you're in a difficult season, but it's essential to have faith in the process. Nature teaches us that periods of stillness or struggle are temporary. They're necessary parts of the cycle that lead to renewal and growth. Even when you can't see it, beneath the surface, things are happening. Roots are growing stronger, and the foundation for your next bloom is being laid.

When spring comes, the trees don't question whether they will bloom; they simply do, as is their nature. Trust that you, too, will bloom in your own time. Life has its ups and downs, but just as the earth knows how to bring the flowers back each spring, your spirit knows how to find renewal. It's part of who you are. You've bloomed before, and you will again.

During this season of waiting or hardship, it's important to remain hopeful and kind to yourself. Use this time to nurture your inner strength, just as trees take in what they need during winter. Take care of yourself, rest, and trust the process. When the time is right, you will emerge from this season stronger and more beautiful than before. The challenges you face now will make your next bloom even more meaningful.

Have faith that good things are coming. Life is full of new beginnings, fresh starts, and opportunities to grow in ways you might not even expect. Just as the flowers return to the earth, your season to bloom will come. It may not happen all at once, and it may not be in the way you envision, but it will come. Hold onto that hope.

Remember, like trees, you are resilient. You have weathered storms before, and you've come through them stronger. You will bloom again, brighter and more vibrant than ever. Trust in the seasons of life, and know that even in your hardest moments, something beautiful is waiting to unfold.

Chapter 9

Maintain your aura

We often focus on external features as the primary definition of beauty, but the reality is that real beauty has much more to do with what lies beneath the surface. It's in the way you handle challenges, the kindness you show others, and the confidence you carry through life. Beauty is shaped by circumstances by the highs and lows, the lessons learned, and the resilience built along the way. Every struggle, every moment of growth, adds depth and richness to who you are, creating qualities that are truly beautiful.

Consider how someone who has faced adversity often carries a quiet strength within them. It's a beauty that comes from having overcome challenges, from having endured and grown. Or think about the warmth and compassion of someone who's spent time caring for others, their energy radiates a beauty that no physical feature can match. These are qualities that can't be seen on the surface, yet they make a person truly beautiful.

Your aura, your energy, this is what draws people to you. It's the confidence you exude, the positivity you share, and the kindness that flows from you. These qualities, built through experience, form the true essence of beauty. They make you stand out in a way that transcends traditional definitions of attractiveness.

The more you embrace who you are and the journey that has shaped you, the more beautiful you become. Beauty isn't something that can be captured in a mirror. It's something you feel in the presence of someone who is authentic, who is comfortable with themselves, and who exudes positivity and strength.

Ultimately, beauty is a reflection of how you carry yourself through life. It's not about perfection or meeting a standard. It's about embodying the qualities that make you unique, the ones that come from everything you've been through and everything you've become. When you understand that beauty is more than skin deep, you start to see it in places you didn't expect, both in yourself and in others.

So, the next time you think about beauty, don't look to the surface. Look at the aura you carry, the energy you bring to the world. That is where true beauty lies, and it's something that only grows stronger with time, experience, and the qualities formed by life's journey.

Change can be painful

Change is painful, but nothing is as painful as staying stuck somewhere you don't belong. The discomfort of remaining in an environment that no longer supports your growth can quietly drain your energy, ambition, and sense of purpose. While change can feel daunting, the alternative, settling for a life that doesn't align with who you truly are, is far more damaging in the long run.

We become the sum of our surroundings, especially the people we spend the most time with. It's often said that "we are the sum of the five people we spend the most time with," and this couldn't be more true. The attitudes, habits, and mindsets of those around us shape who we are becoming, whether we realize it or not. If your environment doesn't inspire growth, you may find yourself adopting the limiting beliefs of those around you, holding yourself back from what you're truly capable of achieving.

If you're surrounded by people who are complacent, negative, or unmotivated, it's easy to stay stuck in that energy. You start to mirror their habits, accepting mediocrity as the norm. The real danger of staying in an environment where you don't belong is that it slowly dulls your potential. Over time, you may feel disconnected from your dreams, or worse, begin to believe that they aren't possible.

On the other hand, when you embrace change, you invite new opportunities for growth. Surrounding yourself with people who inspire, challenge, and uplift you creates a powerful shift in your mindset. You begin to see possibilities where there were once limitations. The friction you once felt in a stagnant environment is replaced by the excitement of moving toward your true potential.

Change isn't easy because it often requires stepping into the unknown. It can be uncomfortable to leave behind familiar routines, relationships, or environments, but that discomfort is temporary. Growth always requires some level of discomfort, but it's a small price to pay for a life that feels aligned with who you are and what you truly want.

It's important to recognize that staying where you don't belong is far more painful in the long run than the temporary discomfort of change. When you embrace change, you take control of your life. You actively seek out environments that support your growth and surround yourself with people who push you to be your best. You stop settling for less and start pursuing more.

So, instead of fearing change, see it as an opportunity to become who you're meant to be. Change is what unlocks your potential, opens new doors, and creates space for you to evolve. While the process may be uncomfortable at first, the rewards are worth it. By embracing change, you're choosing to live a life that's more aligned with your values, your goals, and your true self.

In the end, the choice is clear: you can stay stuck, or you can embrace change. The pain of staying stagnant will always be greater than the discomfort of growth. Change is not something to fear, but something to welcome. It's the only way to truly step into the life you're meant to live.

Embrace differences

It is easy to jump to conclusions or assume that the way we see things is the only way, but that can lead to misunderstandings and a limited view of the world. We often forget that everyone's perspective is shaped by their own experiences, and what seems obvious to one person might look completely different to another. When we approach situations with the belief that our view is the only "right" one, we miss the opportunity to truly understand others.

By considering different perspectives, we can develop a well-rounded view of life. When you listen to others, especially when their views differ from your own, you allow yourself to grow. You begin to see the world through their eyes, gaining insight into their struggles, joys, and reasoning. This doesn't mean you have to agree with everyone, but it helps you approach situations with more compassion and openness.

Imagine how much better the world would be if, instead of rushing to judge, we all paused to ask, "What might this person be experiencing? How does their background shape their point of view?" This simple act of consideration can deepen your understanding of others, strengthen relationships, and create more meaningful connections.

Empathy is the key to bridging the gap between our differences. While we may all share similar emotions fear, joy, love, pain how we experience these feelings is influenced by our personal stories. Taking the time to recognize this helps us move beyond superficial judgments and appreciate the complexity of human experience. When we approach others with empathy, we create space for dialogue, learning, and mutual respect.

Understanding that everyone sees the world differently also enriches your own perspective. When you open yourself to new ideas and viewpoints, you challenge your own assumptions and beliefs. This can lead to personal growth, a broader understanding of life, and a more fulfilling way of interacting with the world. You'll find that your perspective of life shifts in ways you may not have anticipated, opening doors to new possibilities.

So, before jumping to conclusions, take a moment to step back and consider: what might the other person be seeing that you are not? How might their experiences shape their view? By practicing empathy and understanding, you not only connect better with others, but you also allow yourself to see the world in a richer, more meaningful way.

Everyone has two eyes, but we each have our own unique view of life. Embracing this difference, rather than resisting it, brings us closer to the shared humanity that connects us all.

Chapter 10

Minds are magnets

Our minds are magnets. Whatever we think about, we attract. The thoughts you hold, whether positive or negative, have a way of shaping your reality. The external world is often a mirror reflecting your internal world. What you focus on in your mind becomes the energy you put out into the world, and in return, that energy shapes your experiences.

When you fill your mind with thoughts of possibility, growth, and positivity, you begin to see opportunities where others see obstacles. Your mind, like a magnet, attracts the very things you dwell on. If you believe in abundance, you'll find yourself in situations where abundance flows. If you focus on solutions, you'll attract answers. On the other hand, if your thoughts are filled with doubt, fear, and negativity, you'll find that life seems to echo those feelings back to you. You start noticing the challenges more than the possibilities, and your perception of the world becomes clouded by the negativity you are internally nurturing.

Imagine waking up each day believing that things will go wrong, that success is out of reach, or that people are against you. Your mind will latch onto every misstep, every rejection, and every challenge as proof that your thoughts were right. Your external world will mirror that inner belief, reinforcing the negativity and creating a cycle that's hard to break.

Now, imagine waking up believing in the possibility of the day ahead that something good is coming, that you're capable, and that the world is full of opportunity. You'll start to see small moments of progress, little victories, and kindness in the world. The external world will begin to reflect the positive energy you carry within, and life will feel like it's moving in your favour.

The connection between your internal thoughts and your external reality is undeniable. We often underestimate how much our thoughts shape not only our perspective but also the outcomes in our lives. If you think of your mind as a magnet, you'll begin to see how crucial it is to be mindful of what you focus on. The thoughts you allow to dominate your mind create the energy you attract, and that energy shapes your reality.

This isn't just about positive thinking; it's about realizing that your mindset has the power to transform your life. The world around you reacts to the energy you put out. The more you focus on growth, the more opportunities for growth you'll attract. The more you dwell on negativity, the more negativity you'll invite into your life.

The power lies in being conscious of your thoughts and how they influence the world you experience. You don't have to let your mind dwell on fear or doubt. You have the power to shift your focus toward what you want to attract, and by doing so, you begin to change the way you interact with the world.

When you start to see the external world as a reflection of your internal thoughts, you realize the importance of cultivating a mindset that serves you. The power is within you to choose thoughts that align with the life you want to create. Let your mind become a magnet for joy, success, and abundance. The more you focus on those things, the more they will naturally flow into your life.

The energy of your thoughts is real, and it draws similar energy from the world around you. By transforming your internal world, you transform your external experience.

Earn with your mind

For many of us, the notion that success only comes through hard work and sacrifice is deeply ingrained. We are taught to believe that in order to achieve what we want, we must put in long hours, work tirelessly, and trade our time and energy for every ounce of success. This belief can become an invisible trap, holding us back from realizing the full capacity of our minds. The truth is, while effort and commitment are important, your true power doesn't lie in how many hours you work it lies in how you think, create, and leverage your mind.

The idea that you must struggle and sacrifice to succeed often leads to burnout, frustration, and a sense of powerlessness. Many people spend years working tirelessly, yet they feel stuck in the same place. They trade their time for money, thinking that the harder they work, the closer they'll get to their dreams. But this way of thinking is an illusion. While hard work can produce results, it's not the only path and certainly not the most efficient one. The real key to success lies in shifting your mindset and tapping into the power of your mind.

Your mind has the ability to generate ideas, innovate, and create solutions that can change your life. When you start earning with your mind, you stop trading time for money and start creating value. Value comes from your ideas, your creativity, and your ability to solve problems in ways that others haven't yet thought of. This is where true wealth and success are found, not in working endless hours but in thinking smarter, seeing opportunities where others don't, and using your skills in ways that multiply your impact.

Consider the most successful people in any field. They didn't reach the top by working longer hours than everyone else. They got there by using their minds differently. They understood that time is limited, but ideas and creativity are limitless. They found ways to maximize their results by leveraging their thinking, not just their time. Instead of seeing work as a grind, they viewed it as an opportunity to think bigger, to innovate, and to create something valuable.

You have the same capacity within you. Your mind is your most powerful tool, far more valuable than the hours in your day. The more you focus on developing and using your mental capacity, through learning, innovating, and thinking creatively, the less you'll feel like you need to sacrifice your time to get what you want. When you focus on earning with your mind, you shift from a mindset of scarcity, where time is limited and work feels like a constant grind, to one of abundance, where your ideas can create limitless possibilities.

The misconception that you must work hard and sacrifice to succeed is a trap that keeps you focused on what you lack rather than what you already have. The belief that success is only achieved through sacrifice leads to an endless cycle of overwork and dissatisfaction. But once you realize that you can earn with your mind, by using your creativity, problem-solving skills, and unique perspective, you break free from that illusion. You stop thinking in terms of hours worked and start thinking in terms of value created.

When you begin to understand the power of your mind, you see that you can create the life you want without sacrificing everything in the process. You can start a business, pursue a passion, or develop a skill that allows you to provide value to the world, and in return, you'll see success flow back to you. This doesn't mean you don't put in effort or that success is effortless, but it does mean that the effort you put in is focused, meaningful, and driven by your ideas rather than just your time.

You have the capacity to do anything you want, to create any life you desire. The only thing standing in your way is the belief that you have to work harder, longer, and sacrifice more than everyone else to get there. Let go of that belief, and start trusting in the power of your mind. The moment you do, you'll realize that the path to success doesn't require endless sacrifice. It requires vision, creativity, and the ability to see beyond the limits of time. You already have everything you need within you. Use your mind, and you can do anything.

Discuss ideas

Most people, quite frankly, only engage in conversations to hear their own voice echoed back to them. They're not genuinely interested in learning, expanding their minds, or contributing anything of real value. Their words lack depth, their points of view are predictable, and their discussions circle around the mundane and irrelevant.

Let's face it: the majority of people settle for talking about trivial matters, gossip, social events, what they watched on TV last night. These conversations have no substance. They fill the air with words that do nothing more than pass the time, all while pretending to engage. They ask questions without waiting for real answers and respond without understanding. Their exchanges are shallow because they are not driven by curiosity or the pursuit of truth, but by the need to occupy space.

The truth is, people who engage at that level never rise above mediocrity. They stay within their comfort zone, discussing matters that keep them intellectually stagnant. When their conversations revolve around others, what someone wore, what they said, how they acted, it becomes clear they're too small-minded to discuss real ideas. They don't challenge themselves, because they simply don't have the capacity to. They avoid discussing ideas because ideas require thought, consideration, and often a level of introspection that they're simply not equipped for.

It's no surprise that they find themselves surrounded by mediocrity. People of substance don't waste their time entertaining small talk or idle gossip. Their minds are engaged in more important things, big ideas, ground breaking innovations, philosophical questions that challenge the status quo. These are the conversations that shape the future, and it's no coincidence that they're held by the few who are capable of thinking at a higher level.

So the next time you find yourself in a conversation, observe closely. Most are simply talking to fill a void, responding out of obligation rather than intention. They skim the surface of topics because it's easier, safer, and requires little from them. It's a reflection of their intellectual laziness. Don't be fooled into thinking there's value in such exchanges. Seek conversations with people who understand the weight of their words and the power of ideas.

Chapter 11

Think differently

Not all thoughts that cross your mind belong to you. We often fall into the trap of assuming that every thought we have is a reflection of who we are. But in reality, many of the thoughts that come and go are shaped by external influences, society, media, family, friends, and even the culture we grew up in. We absorb these ideas subconsciously, and over time, they blend with our own internal voice, making it hard to distinguish which thoughts are truly ours and which have been planted there.

Identifying too closely with your thoughts can create a false sense of restriction. You begin to believe that your inner dialogue is the final word on who you are and what you can achieve. But this assumption is far from the truth. Your thoughts are just one small part of your overall consciousness, they don't define you. When you realize that not all your thoughts are truly yours, you can start to take a step back and view them objectively.

Thoughts can be automatic, often reacting to things we've experienced, seen, or been told. For instance, have you ever caught yourself thinking something negative about your abilities, even when deep down you know it's not true? Or maybe you've judged yourself harshly based on societal standards that don't align with your values. These are just examples of how thoughts can stem from places other than your authentic self.

The danger of identifying too closely with your thoughts is that it can limit your potential. When you assume every thought is yours, you might feel restricted by the meaning behind your words or ideas. You might believe you're only capable of what your inner dialogue suggests, or worse, that you must act according to every thought that crosses your mind. But this assumption overlooks a critical truth: you are the thinker of your thoughts, not the thoughts themselves.

When you start observing your thoughts without automatically accepting them, you open up space for growth and clarity. You can challenge thoughts that limit you, question the ones that make you feel small, and discard those that don't serve your purpose. This awareness allows you to choose which thoughts are worth nurturing and which ones are simply noise.

Think of your mind as a vast landscape of ideas, only some of which truly belong to you. By filtering through these thoughts, you can identify the ones that resonate with your true self and allow them to guide your actions and decisions. The rest, the thoughts that create doubt, fear, or limitation, can be let go, as they aren't rooted in your authentic nature.

By thinking differently, you begin to understand that you are much more than your thoughts. You are the observer, the one who has the power to shape which ideas define your reality. This shift in perspective frees you from being confined by old, limiting thoughts and opens the door to a deeper connection with your true potential.

When you recognize that not all thoughts are yours, you gain the freedom to create your own meaning, your own narrative, and your own reality. This awareness gives you the power to redefine who you are, unbound by the restrictions of your automatic inner dialogue. Instead, you can consciously choose the thoughts that elevate you and lead you toward a life aligned with your true self.

Shifting mindset

Approaching life with the mindset that you have the capacity to achieve everything you want creates a powerful shift. It's not about wishful thinking or blind optimism; it's about opening yourself up to possibilities and believing that you're capable of achieving more. This mindset invites the right opportunities, people, and circumstances into your life, helping to turn your desires into reality.

When you truly believe that you can have everything you want, you start seeing opportunities where others see limitations. Your focus changes from what you don't have to what you can create. This change in perspective empowers you to take action, because you're no longer weighed down by doubt or fear. You begin to approach life with a sense of purpose and confidence, knowing that whatever you need to achieve your goals will come to you in time.

Believing in your capacity also shifts how others perceive you. People are naturally drawn to those who have a clear vision for their lives and the confidence to pursue it. You may find yourself surrounded by people who support your growth, offer guidance, or present opportunities that align with your goals. The energy you put out into the world, one of capability and possibility, attracts the resources and connections you need to succeed.

This perspective also has a profound impact on your decision-making. When you believe you're capable of having what you want, you stop settling for less. You no longer make choices based on fear of failure or lack of options. Instead, you choose paths that align with your higher aspirations, trusting that each step will bring you closer to your goals. This inner confidence allows you to embrace challenges as part of the journey, rather than seeing them as roadblocks.

It's important to understand that approaching life from this perspective doesn't mean everything will come easily or without effort. But when you trust in your ability to have what you desire, the things you need, the right tools, knowledge, and support, will start appearing. They may not always come in the form you expect, but they will align with your journey, helping you grow and move forward.

So, as you move through life, try shifting your mindset. Instead of focusing on what you lack or what seems impossible, start believing that you have the capacity to achieve everything you want. This belief will invite the resources, opportunities, and people you need into your life. With that mindset, you're no longer just reacting to life, you're actively shaping it, creating a path that leads to fulfillment and success.

Choose to evolve

It is easy to get stuck in routines, repeating the same patterns year after year, while hoping for different results. But staying in your comfort zone, where things feel safe and familiar, can hold you back from the true potential life has to offer. When we stay stagnant, we deprive ourselves of growth and the excitement that comes from becoming a better version of ourselves.

Life becomes so much more fulfilling and prosperous when we choose to evolve, when we fall in love with improving ourselves. Self-improvement isn't about perfection, but about continuous progress. It's about being willing to learn, grow, and challenge yourself in new ways. Every small step toward bettering yourself adds to your personal development, opening doors to new opportunities, new mindsets, and ultimately, a richer life experience.

One of the most important things to remember on this journey is that "comparison is the thief of joy". It's easy to look at others and feel as though you're not moving fast enough or achieving enough. But focusing on someone else's journey robs you of the satisfaction of your own progress. Your path is unique, and it doesn't need to look like anyone else's. When you stop comparing and start focusing on your personal growth, you realize how much joy comes from simply being better than you were yesterday.

Think of how much can change when you shift your focus from simply surviving to thriving. When you choose to prioritize your growth, whether it's learning a new skill, improving your health, or working on your mindset, life naturally becomes more exciting. The journey of self-improvement is filled with moments of discovery, about yourself, your abilities, and the endless possibilities ahead.

Falling in love with self-improvement also teaches you to appreciate the process, not just the end result. It's not about overnight success; it's about committing to being better than you were yesterday. With every bit of progress, your confidence grows, and you start to realize that you are capable of more than you ever thought. You begin to feel proud of your efforts, even when the journey gets tough, because you know you're moving in the right direction.

When you invest in yourself and your growth, prosperity follows naturally. This doesn't just mean financial prosperity, though that can certainly be a part of it. It's about overall abundance, emotional, mental, and even spiritual. You become more open to new experiences, new people, and new ways of thinking. Your relationships improve, your career advances, and your general outlook on life becomes more positive. Success in all areas starts from within.

So, instead of allowing another year to pass by without change, commit to evolving. Take the leap and invest in your personal growth. Let go of the belief that you need to wait for the right moment or that life will somehow magically change for the better without your active participation. Start today. Challenge yourself to step out of your comfort zone and embrace the idea of becoming a better version of yourself.

When you fall in love with improving yourself, and stop comparing yourself to others, you'll find that life becomes far more rewarding, filled with excitement, opportunity, and growth. Don't wait. Evolve, and watch how life unfolds in ways you never imagined.

Chapter 12

Limitless possibilities

Our reality is determined by ourselves alone. Whether we realize it or not, we are constantly shaping the world we live in with our thoughts, choices, and beliefs. The power to create the life you want is entirely in your hands, and understanding this truth is the first step to unlocking your potential.

It is easy to think that life just happens to us, that circumstances beyond our control dictate our happiness or success. But the truth is, how we choose to interpret, respond, and act in any given situation determines our reality. You are not powerless in the face of challenges, nor are you bound by limitations others might impose on you. The reality you live in today is a result of the choices you've made, the beliefs you hold, and the actions you've taken.

Once you understand this, you begin to see how much control you really have. Your thoughts shape your mindset, and your mindset shapes your actions. If you believe that you can achieve something, you're far more likely to take steps toward making it happen. On the other hand, if you tell yourself that success is out of reach, you'll unconsciously create barriers that keep you from achieving it.

You have the power to do whatever you want, and it all starts with recognizing that you are the author of your own story. Every choice, every decision, every action moves you closer to the reality you want to create. Don't let external circumstances or the opinions of others convince you that you are limited. You are capable of far more than you know, and the life you envision for yourself is within reach, as long as you believe in your ability to create it.

When you realize that your reality is shaped by your mindset and actions, you reclaim your power. You no longer have to wait for permission, validation, or the "right" moment to pursue your dreams. You can start now, with whatever resources or tools you have, and build from there. The possibilities are endless, but they only become real when you decide to make them so.

By shifting your mindset, recognising your power, and taking intentional steps, you can transform your life. You have the freedom to choose your path, to pursue your passions, and to create a reality that aligns with who you truly are. This is your life, and the power to shape it is entirely yours.

So, embrace the fact that you are in control. Your reality is not something that happens to you, it's something you create. You have the power to do whatever you want, and once you fully understand that, the possibilities for your life become limitless.

Embrace discomfort

If you are healing and breaking all at once, do not fear, this is growth. You have the power to transform your discomfort into something far greater.

Life often puts us in situations where we feel like we're both falling apart and mending simultaneously. These moments can be confusing, even painful, but they are also powerful. Growth is never easy or smooth, and often the discomfort you feel is a sign that you are evolving in ways you can't yet fully see. The breaking is necessary for something new and stronger to emerge. It's in these moments of feeling torn apart that your greatest transformations are born.

What you might not realize is that you hold the power to transmute this discomfort. It doesn't have to stay as pain. You can take the energy of what you're going through and turn it into something meaningful, something that brings you closer to who you're meant to be. When you feel broken, it's easy to assume the pain is all there is, but underneath that discomfort lies the potential for strength, wisdom, and growth. You have the ability to take those feelings of unraveling and channel them into your healing process.

Growth is uncomfortable by nature because it pushes us beyond what we know and into new territory. But discomfort doesn't mean you're stuck; it means you're moving. You are shifting, evolving, becoming something more. It's in this uncomfortable space where you hold the power to decide what happens next. Will you let the pain consume you, or will you take that discomfort and transform it into fuel for your growth?

Empathize with yourself, but also recognize your own strength. You are not merely at the mercy of your circumstances. Even in the hardest moments, you have the power to reshape how you experience them. This is not to say the pain will disappear overnight, it won't. But your ability to transmute that discomfort into something greater gives you control over your path. Pain is temporary, but the lessons you take from it, and the growth it spurs, are lasting.

As you go through your stages of growth, remind yourself that this process is yours to own. You are not powerless in the face of discomfort. You are, in fact, in the middle of one of the most powerful shifts you'll experience. By embracing this discomfort, you can shape it into something that serves you. The energy of pain, uncertainty, and fear can be alchemized into resilience, strength, and clarity. You hold that power.

So, if you're healing and breaking at the same time, know that this is growth, and more importantly, that you are capable of turning that discomfort into something greater. You have the strength to transmute pain into progress, to turn fear into fuel for transformation. Trust in your ability to rise from these moments stronger, wiser, and more aligned with who you are meant to be. You are not defined by the breaking; you are defined by how you rebuild.

Embracing the truth

When we speak the truth, we've done nothing but allow things to follow their natural course, because nature itself is the embodiment of truth. Just as trees grow, rivers flow, and the sun rises each day without pretence, the truth exists as a fundamental force that requires no embellishment or manipulation. To live in truth is to align ourselves with the natural order of the world, where everything is as it should be, unburdened by falsehoods or illusions.

Nature offers us a profound lesson in authenticity. In the natural world, there are no masks or pretensions. A flower doesn't attempt to be something it's not, nor does the ocean pretend to be calm when it's turbulent. Everything in nature is true to itself, and it exists in perfect balance because of this. When we speak the truth, we honour that same sense of authenticity in our own lives, letting go of the need to control outcomes or craft false realities. Instead, we allow life to unfold as it is meant to, trusting in the natural course of events.

When we choose honesty, we are not forcing something unnatural; we are simply letting things flow. In doing so, we open the door to clarity, understanding, and genuine connection. Truth has a way of cutting through confusion and aligning people and situations with reality. Lies, on the other hand, act as obstructions temporary barriers that may seem to serve a purpose in the short term but inevitably disrupt the natural balance. They lead to misunderstanding, mistrust, and ultimately greater chaos. But truth, like a flowing river, clears the path and allows things to progress naturally.

The power of truth lies in its simplicity and resilience. It doesn't need to be explained or justified. It simply is. Just as nature persists through storms, droughts, and disruptions, truth endures, no matter how much it is suppressed or ignored. When we speak the truth, even when it's difficult, we tap into this enduring power. It may not always produce immediate results or bring instant comfort, but in the long run, it creates harmony and balance. Truth has a way of restoring what has been thrown off course, much like how nature eventually restores balance after disruption.

This idea of truth following a natural course also extends to our relationships. When we are truthful with ourselves and with others, we cultivate trust and respect. People are drawn to honesty because it creates a space where real connection can grow. Lies, even small ones, create cracks in the foundation of relationships. They introduce doubt, making it difficult to trust fully. But when we speak the truth, we allow relationships to develop in a way that is genuine and stable. There is no need for guesswork or second-guessing because what is said is what is real.

Being truthful also means we stop trying to control everything around us. Many times, we hide the truth because we fear what will happen if it's revealed. We worry about losing control over situations, or we fear the consequences of honesty. But when we speak the truth, we release that control. We trust that life, much like nature, has a way of working things out when we are aligned with honesty. This doesn't mean the road will always be easy, but it does mean that the path we walk will be real, and ultimately more fulfilling.

Truth, like nature, is often patient. It doesn't always yield immediate results or bring about instant resolutions, but it is steady. Speaking the truth may cause discomfort or disrupt the status quo, but over time, it leads to growth, healing, and resolution. Just as nature requires time to heal after a storm or adjust after a change, truth also needs time to unfold and reveal its benefits. But in the end, it brings balance back to our lives.

In embracing truth, we allow things to follow their natural course. We let go of the illusions that hold us back and trust in the strength of authenticity. Nature shows us that the truth is always there, waiting to be acknowledged and embraced. By speaking the truth, we align ourselves with that deeper, natural order, letting life flow in its most harmonious and genuine form.

Chapter 13

Stay away from negativity

Negative people have a problem for every solution. This type of mindset, often called a "negative bias," causes individuals to focus on what could go wrong, rather than seeing the possibilities for improvement. No matter how constructive or well-intentioned a solution might be, negative people tend to find a flaw or an obstacle. This constant tendency to criticize or dismiss solutions can be incredibly draining not only for the person stuck in this mindset but also for those around them who are trying to encourage growth, progress, or change.

One of the most frustrating things about dealing with someone who is always negative is that it feels like you're running into a brick wall. You might offer a thoughtful solution to a problem or suggest a positive path forward, but they immediately counter with all the reasons why it won't work. It's as if their focus is solely on finding the downsides or obstacles, rather than giving the solution a fair chance. This behaviour often comes from a place of fear, self-doubt, or past experiences where they've been let down. However, it ultimately prevents any real progress from happening.

When someone is constantly focused on what's wrong, they trap themselves and others into a cycle of inaction. They resist solutions because they've already convinced themselves that it won't make a difference. This mindset can permeate many areas of life, whether it's in relationships, work, or personal challenges. By always focusing on problems, negative people not only block their own growth but also discourage those around them from trying to move forward. It's as if they are so invested in maintaining the status quo, no matter how unhappy it makes them, that they reject any chance for improvement.

This attitude can be toxic in group settings, whether in a family, workplace, or friendship circle. Negativity has a way of spreading, and before long, it becomes the dominant tone of the group. Creative ideas are shot down, optimism is stifled, and the energy to tackle challenges with enthusiasm is diminished. When every solution is met with a problem, people stop trying to come up with answers because it feels pointless. The space for innovation, growth, and possibility shrinks.

Negative people are often not aware of the impact their mindset has on themselves and others. While their constant focus on problems might come from a place of caution or fear of failure, they fail to see that it actually perpetuates the very issues they are trying to avoid. Solutions are supposed to solve problems, but when viewed through a negative lens, they only become more obstacles to overcome. This creates a loop of negativity, where nothing feels like it will ever get better.

It's important to recognize this in both others and ourselves. At times, we all have moments where we feel pessimistic or overwhelmed by challenges. However, consistently adopting this mindset can prevent progress in life. While it's natural to acknowledge risks or difficulties, being stuck in a negative loop of always seeing problems instead of possibilities is counterproductive.

Adopting a more positive, solution-oriented mindset can change everything. Instead of dwelling on why something might not work, we can choose to focus on how to make it work. This shift in perspective fosters resilience and adaptability. It encourages us to see challenges not as immovable roadblocks but as opportunities for growth. This doesn't mean we ignore potential risks or difficulties; it simply means we approach them with a more balanced, hopeful attitude.

Surrounding yourself with people who have a more solution-oriented mindset can also have a powerful effect. When you're with others who are focused on progress, you feel more energized and motivated to tackle challenges. Together, you find ways to overcome obstacles and turn problems into possibilities. Encouraging this mindset in yourself and those around you creates an environment where progress is not only possible but also sustainable.

In the end, the way we view challenges and solutions greatly impacts our ability to move forward in life. Those who choose to focus on possibilities instead of problems create space for growth and success.

On the other hand, those who constantly find issues in every solution only limit themselves. By shifting from a problem-focused mindset to one that embraces solutions, we open ourselves up to new opportunities and a more fulfilling path forward.

We cannot force people

We can't force people to choose us. No matter how much we want someone's affection, approval, or attention, trying to impose our will on others only pushes them further away. True connections, whether in friendships, relationships, or any aspect of life, are built on mutual understanding and choice. Forcing or pressuring others into choosing us leads to shallow, unsustainable relationships that lack the genuine affection or respect needed to thrive. The best connections are those that come from a place of free will where the other person chooses us not because they were coerced, but because they genuinely want to be in our lives.

It's natural to want to be chosen. We all long for validation, whether it's from a romantic partner, a friend, or even in a work setting. When we feel strongly about someone, the temptation to control their decision, to make them see our value, can be overwhelming. But trying to control someone's choice whether through manipulation, guilt, or persistent persuasion usually backfires. Instead of drawing someone closer, this behaviour pushes them away. People naturally resist being told what to feel or how to act. Imposing our will disrupts the organic flow of the relationship and erodes trust.

True affection or loyalty can't be forced. When someone chooses us freely, it's because they've seen our value on their own terms. They've made the decision without pressure, and that choice is far more powerful than one that's coerced. The more we try to control others, the more they pull away, sensing that their autonomy is being threatened. For any relationship to be meaningful, the other person must have the space to come to their own conclusions. They must feel free to choose, without feeling like they're being influenced or manipulated into doing so.

By giving people the space to choose on their own, we allow relationships to be built on genuine connection, not obligation. When someone chooses to be with us whether it's as a partner, a friend, or a collaborator it means so much more because it's authentic. There's no doubt or second-guessing, and the relationship has the foundation of trust and mutual respect.

It's also important to understand that not everyone will choose us, and that's okay. Part of living authentically means accepting that we won't always be everyone's first choice. This doesn't diminish our worth. In fact, it's freeing to know that we don't need to constantly seek approval or force connections. When we focus on being ourselves and respecting the autonomy of others, the right people will naturally gravitate toward us. They'll choose us because they see something real, something valuable, without any external pressure.

The best things in life come from genuine, unforced choices. When people freely decide to be part of our lives, the relationship feels more fulfilling, more sustainable, and more meaningful. By letting go of the need to control how others feel or act, we open the door to connections that are based on real desire and mutual respect. Those are the relationships that last the ones built on the solid ground of freedom, choice, and authenticity.

So, it's crucial to resist the urge to impose our will on others. When we give them the space to choose on their own terms, without pressure or manipulation, we set the stage for deeper, more meaningful connections. True relationships blossom when they are free from external influence, and those who choose us of their own accord will bring a greater sense of joy and fulfillment into our lives.

Choosing to leave

The best relationships are built on mutual respect, understanding, and reciprocity. You deserve to be in connections where your time, energy, and love are not only valued but returned. It's easy to forget this when someone makes you feel like you're just a backup plan or a convenience. But here's the truth: you're worth so much more than that. You deserve relationships where you're treated as a priority, not an afterthought, and where the effort is shared.

Reciprocal relationships create balance. In these connections, both parties invest equally in the relationship, whether it's emotional support, time, or effort. You're not constantly giving while the other person only takes. Instead, you both uplift and encourage one another, growing stronger together. These are the relationships that make you feel seen, valued, and confident in who you are.

When you're in a reciprocal relationship, you're reminded of your own worth. There's no need to chase validation or wonder where you stand. The people who truly value you will show it in their actions, not just in words. They will make time for you, listen to you, and support your growth, just as you do for them. This mutual care is the foundation of the best relationships.

Confidence comes when you realize you deserve this kind of reciprocity. You don't have to settle for less or accept being treated like an option. You're worthy of relationships that make you feel good, that enhance your life rather than drain it. Trust in your ability to attract people who see your worth and treat you accordingly. When you do, you'll find yourself surrounded by those who genuinely care about you, and who match your effort with their own.

Remember, relationships that are one-sided or imbalanced only bring frustration and self-doubt. But when you know your worth, you no longer feel the need to chase those who don't see it. You step into relationships where you are met with the same level of care and attention that you give, and that's where your confidence will grow.

You have the power to choose who gets to be in your life, and those who treat you like an option don't deserve a place in it. By embracing relationships that are reciprocal, you are choosing connections that reflect your value. You are worthy of this, and you deserve nothing less.

So, trust in yourself. The best relationships are those that give as much as they receive, and you are fully deserving of relationships that bring out the best in you. Confidence isn't about proving your worth to others, it is about knowing that you're worth the effort and care of those who see you as a priority.

Chapter 14

No one is perfect

No one in this world is pure and perfect. Every person you meet has flaws, makes mistakes, and carries the weight of their own experiences. If you choose to avoid people because of their imperfections, you will find yourself walking through life alone. True, lasting relationships are not built on the expectation of perfection, but on the acceptance of each other's humanity. The key to meaningful connection is learning to embrace people for who they are, not for who you want them to be.

We often have an idealised version of what people should be like whether it's a friend who never disappoints us, a partner who always understands us, or a family member who never makes mistakes. But the reality is that this idealized version of perfection doesn't exist. People are messy, complex, and fallible. If you hold on to the belief that people must meet your ideal expectations, you'll constantly find yourself disappointed and distanced from those around you.

Acceptance is the foundation of real relationships. It's about seeing someone for all that they are, their strengths, their weaknesses, their struggles, and their achievements and loving them anyway. It doesn't mean turning a blind eye to hurtful behaviour or unhealthy patterns, but it does mean allowing people the space to be imperfect without constantly judging them for it. When you accept people as they are, you build deeper, more authentic connections because those relationships are based on reality, not some fantasy version of what you think they should be.

Expecting perfection from others is not only unfair, but it's also isolating. When you constantly focus on the flaws in the people around you, you overlook their good qualities. This mindset can make you hypercritical and distant, always seeking reasons to pull away rather than appreciating the ways they enrich your life. Real connection comes when you let go of those impossible standards and allow people to be human flawed but still worthy of love and respect.

By accepting others for who they are, you also learn to practice compassion and empathy. Everyone has bad days, moments of weakness, and times when they don't live up to their best selves. Just as you make mistakes and grow from them, so do the people around you. Accepting this reality encourages a more compassionate perspective one that acknowledges that people are doing their best, even if they sometimes fall short. This shift in perspective not only strengthens your relationships but also helps you become a more patient and understanding person.

Additionally, accepting others as they are helps you let go of the need for control. Often, our desire for others to be a certain way comes from wanting to control the outcome of our interactions and relationships. We want people to fit into our expectations to feel safe, secure, and validated. However, this mindset creates a rigid and stressful environment, both for ourselves and those around us. When you release the need to control others, you open yourself up to deeper, more flexible relationships. You begin to appreciate people for their unique contributions to your life, rather than constantly measuring them against an unrealistic standard.

Avoiding people because of their mistakes leads to loneliness and missed opportunities for growth. Relationships are a two-way street, and part of that is learning to accept that everyone including yourself is imperfect. When you realize that no one will ever meet every expectation you have, it frees you from the disappointment and frustration that comes from chasing perfection. Instead, you can focus on what truly matters: shared experiences, mutual support, and the ability to grow together, flaws and all.

Relationships are most fulfilling when they are built on acceptance, not unrealistic ideals. Letting go of the need for perfection allows you to experience deeper, more genuine connections with the people around you. It allows relationships to grow through the challenges and mistakes, rather than being stifled by them. If you spend your time avoiding people for their flaws, you may end up alone. But if you learn to accept and appreciate people as they are, imperfections and all, you open yourself up to the rich, fulfilling connections that make life meaningful.

Pursue your future

Do not let the past stop you from finding the success, joy, or purpose that awaits you. It is easy to become discouraged after facing rejection, disappointment, or struggles. When you put your heart and effort into something, only to see it not turn out the way you hoped, the natural instinct is to withdraw, to protect yourself from future pain. But these experiences are not signs that you should stop trying, they are part of your journey, shaping you for something bigger.

Every challenge you face is preparing you for what's to come. The times when things didn't work out, when you felt defeated or unworthy, weren't moments to define your limits, they were moments designed to build your resilience. They teach you more about your inner strength, refining your skills and sharpening your vision for what truly matters. Success, fulfillment, and purpose do not come without moments of failure or struggle. It's within these tough moments that you grow the most.

When things don't go as planned, the temptation to pull back is strong. You might think it's safer to stay in your comfort zone, to avoid further risks. But in doing so, you may also miss out on incredible opportunities. The universe often tests us through setbacks to see how committed we are to our own potential. Every failed attempt or challenge is a necessary step toward eventual success. These experiences are like the foundation being laid, and although the process might be slow or painful, it is creating the strength you'll need to hold up the weight of future triumphs.

The key is to not let these moments of discouragement make you believe that you're not capable or that success is out of reach. The truth is, no one achieves anything meaningful without encountering roadblocks along the way. Those setbacks are the very things that make future victories sweeter. They allow you to appreciate the process, to understand the value of perseverance, and to grow into the person who can handle the success you're aiming for.

If you retreat now, you risk cutting yourself off from the very experiences that could lead to your greatest achievements. Life's journey is not about avoiding discomfort or challenges, but about learning how to navigate them with grace and determination. Each obstacle is not the end, it is a building block toward your ultimate goals. The more you face them head-on, the more prepared you become for what's to come.

Remember, the road to success and fulfillment is rarely smooth. It's full of twists, turns, and setbacks that feel overwhelming in the moment. But if you keep moving forward, if you refuse to let past disappointments hold you back, you'll discover that every struggle was pushing you toward something greater. The very experiences that once felt like failures will become the stepping stones to your best self.

So, don't let the difficulties of the past stop you from pursuing your future. Every moment, whether a success or a setback, is part of a greater plan, working in harmony to prepare you for something better. Stay open, stay committed, and trust that the challenges you face today are simply making you stronger for the opportunities that lie ahead. Your journey is still unfolding, and there is so much more waiting for you if you remain open to it.

Always be humble

Always be humble, because what God gives, He can also take away. Life is filled with blessings opportunities, relationships, success that often feel like gifts meant to enrich our lives. But it's important to remember that these blessings are not guaranteed to last forever. Humility reminds us to appreciate what we have without taking it for granted, understanding that the same forces that provide can also take away.

When we remain humble, we acknowledge that much of what we achieve or receive is not solely the result of our own efforts. While hard work and perseverance are important, there are factors beyond our control timing, luck, divine intervention that contribute to our success. Recognizing this keeps us grounded and grateful. It helps us avoid the pitfalls of arrogance or entitlement, ensuring that we stay connected to our values rather than becoming overly attached to our achievements or possessions.

Humility also fosters gratitude. When you are humble, you don't view life's blessings as something you are owed, but rather as gifts to be cherished. You appreciate the present moment, recognizing the fragility of the things you value most. This mindset allows you to live more fully, savouring life's blessings without the fear of losing them but with the understanding that nothing is permanent.

In times of abundance, humility encourages generosity and kindness. It reminds us to share our blessings with others and not to let success inflate our ego. By staying humble, we avoid the trap of looking down on others or assuming we are better because of what we've gained. Instead, we remain focused on using our blessings to uplift those around us, knowing that the wheel of fortune can turn for anyone at any time.

Humility also helps us navigate loss with grace. When life changes and what was once given is taken away, humility allows us to adapt and reflect, rather than feeling devastated or resentful. It prepares us for the ups and downs of life, keeping us grounded in the understanding that all things are temporary.

In the end, humility is a reminder to cherish what we have, remain grateful, and use our blessings wisely. Life's gifts are precious, but they are also fleeting, and humility helps us appreciate them fully while they last.

Chapter 15

Don't attach yourself

When you attach yourself to things of genuine value, you experience growth, fulfilment, and a deep sense of purpose. Whether it's nurturing relationships that inspire and support you, dedicating yourself to personal growth, or pursuing passions that align with your true self, these are the things that offer lasting satisfaction. They help you move forward, build resilience, and find joy in life's journey. The value they bring isn't fleeting, it is profound and enriching, guiding you to a more meaningful existence.

In contrast, when you invest your time and energy into things that don't uplift you whether it's toxic relationships, harmful behaviours, or negative mindsets these attachments drain you over time. They pull you away from your potential and leave you feeling depleted. What seems convenient or familiar can eventually erode your confidence, your well-being, and your sense of worth. True value can never be found in things that diminish who you are. These attachments act as weight, holding you back from reaching new heights.

Think about the relationships that truly nourish you. These aren't the ones where you feel pressured, manipulated, or undervalued. They are the ones where you feel seen, appreciated, and supported. They uplift you because they are built on mutual respect, love, and understanding. Such relationships encourage growth, foster self-confidence, and inspire you to be the best version of yourself. You leave these interactions feeling lighter, empowered, and more connected to your true self.

The same goes for the pursuits and passions that truly matter. When you engage in activities that align with your values and purpose, you feel energized, inspired, and fulfilled. These endeavours don't just serve to pass the time, they enrich your life, giving you a sense of accomplishment and joy. Whether it's creative expression, personal growth, or a career with purpose, these are the things that uplift your spirit and give your life real value.

True value is found in things that encourage you to rise above limitations and live authentically. It's found in the people who believe in you, the habits that strengthen you, and the dreams that ignite your passion. When you focus on attaching yourself to what uplifts you, you begin to cultivate a life filled with meaning, joy, and self-respect. You stop chasing after what feels good in the short term and start building a foundation that supports long-term happiness and fulfilment.

To find true value in your life, take a moment to reflect on what truly uplifts you. Are there people, activities, or habits in your life that leave you feeling drained or less than you are? If so, consider letting them go, even if it's difficult. By doing so, you make room for the things that will uplift and support you in the journey ahead. True value isn't found in what weighs you down it's found in what empowers you to grow, thrive, and be at peace with yourself.

Choosing things that uplift you is a conscious decision to prioritize your well-being, your growth, and your happiness. It's recognizing that you deserve to surround yourself with what truly adds value to your life, rather than what takes it away. By seeking out and attaching yourself to these things, you ensure that your life is filled with love, purpose, and genuine fulfilment.

Stop seeking for love

As adults, these early experiences shape how we view relationships and how we seek love. When we're not fed love on a silver spoon as children, we often grow up searching for it in places where it is easily accessible, even if it's not healthy. We might find ourselves drawn to toxic dynamics, repeating patterns of chasing after affection that mirrors the pain and confusion we experienced in our early years. It becomes easy to mistake attention, control, or even manipulation for love because it resembles the only form of care we knew.

Instead of seeking love that nurtures and uplifts us, we may gravitate toward what feels familiar, even if that familiarity comes with emotional wounds. The longing for love remains, but without a clear understanding of what real love should feel like safe, consistent, and kind we accept versions of it that hurt us, mistaking intensity for intimacy or chaos for passion.

The tragic reality is that when we grow up without healthy examples of love, we become conditioned to think that love is something to be earned, fought for, or tolerated in painful forms. We search for it where it's easily accessible, often settling for relationships or situations that offer just a glimmer of affection, even if it's accompanied by harm or neglect.

The key realization is that love shouldn't hurt. Love is not something that should leave us in pieces, always reaching for more but never feeling fully nourished. The journey to healing from this involves unlearning the false beliefs we've internalized about love. It's about recognizing that real love is given freely, without strings attached, and without the need to constantly prove your worth to someone else.

By understanding this, we begin the path to healing, learning that we deserve love that comes without knives, that is soft, kind, and true. This journey allows us to stop searching for love in places where we'll only get hurt and start seeking it in relationships that offer the safety and care we have always needed.

You are loved

One of the purest and most selfless things someone can do is to work on themselves in order to love you the way you deserve to be loved. It's a profound act of love when someone recognizes their own shortcomings or struggles and takes steps to address them, not just for their own benefit, but to be a better partner for you. This kind of effort shows a deep commitment to the relationship and a true desire to give you the kind of love that is thoughtful, self-aware, and nurturing.

When someone chooses to fix themselves whether that means healing from past wounds, developing emotional intelligence, or learning how to communicate better it's a sign that they value the relationship enough to evolve. It's not about being perfect; it's about acknowledging that love, in its truest form, requires growth and the willingness to become the best version of oneself. This act of self-improvement isn't easy, but it's a clear indicator of how much they care about you and the future you're building together.

Often, relationships highlight areas in our lives that need attention. Whether it's learning to be more patient, managing insecurities, or developing better communication skills, these are all part of becoming a more loving, present partner. When someone takes the initiative to address these areas, it means they are thinking about how they can show up for you in the best possible way. They aren't just trying to love you on the surface; they want to love you in a way that meets your emotional, mental, and even spiritual needs.

This process of self-improvement also reflects their deep respect for you. They understand that you deserve a love that is patient, kind, and thoughtful one that comes from a place of stability and emotional maturity. Instead of expecting you to accept their flaws or shortcomings without question, they're making the conscious choice to grow for the sake of the relationship. They want to love you in a way that honours your worth, and that's a truly beautiful thing.

There's something deeply pure about this kind of effort because it's not motivated by obligation or guilt, but by love and respect. When someone loves you enough to fix themselves, they're saying, "You are important to me, and I want to give you the best of myself." They recognize that love isn't static, it's a journey of continuous growth and understanding. By working on themselves, they are actively building a foundation for a stronger, healthier relationship.

In the end, the love you receive from someone who has done the work to improve themselves is richer, deeper, and more meaningful. It's a love that isn't limited by unresolved issues or personal baggage, but one that is grounded in self-awareness and genuine care. They are striving to be the person who can love you exactly how you deserve to be loved fully, deeply, and with all the thoughtfulness that true love requires. And that, in itself, is one of the purest acts of love a person can offer.

Chapter 16

Live in peace

Why do we only wish for people to rest in peace? Why shouldn't they live in peace too? It's a question worth pondering, one that gently nudges us to reflect on how we move through life. So many of us spend our days rushing, struggling, and carrying burdens both visible and invisible waiting for some distant future moment to find peace. But why should peace only be reserved for the end of life? Shouldn't it be something we seek now, something we cultivate in how we live, love, and treat ourselves and others?

We often hear the phrase "Rest in Peace" when someone has passed, as though peace is the final reward after a life of turmoil and effort. But life itself is not meant to be an endless struggle. We don't need to reach the end to deserve peace. Yet, so many of us delay it, thinking peace is only possible once we've solved all our problems, reached every goal, or overcome every obstacle. We live with this idea that peace is something we have to earn, as if it's a prize waiting for us at the finish line.

But what if peace was available to us now? What if we could live in peace, not just hope to rest in it? What would change if we allowed ourselves to let go of the things that weigh us down, fear, resentment, anxiety, and the constant pursuit of more and embraced peace as part of our daily lives? The truth is, peace isn't something that's granted to us only when life is over. It's something we can create, moment by moment, in how we choose to live.

Living in peace doesn't mean life is without challenges or that we will never experience pain. It's not about escaping the difficulties that inevitably come our way. Instead, it's about finding a way to navigate life's storms with a sense of calm and clarity. It's about choosing not to let the chaos of the world dictate our inner state. Peace comes from within, and it begins with the choices we make each day.

So why wait? Why not seek peace today, in this moment? We don't need to solve every problem to deserve peace. We can have peace even in the midst of life's messiness. It's about taking a deep breath, letting go of what we can't control, and finding solace in the present. It's in choosing to forgive, to love, to let go of the past, and to embrace the present with grace and gratitude.

Think about the people you love, the people around you. Wouldn't you want them to live in peace, not just rest in it someday? And wouldn't you want that for yourself? Imagine a world where we prioritize peace while we are still here, alive, breathing. Where peace isn't something we long for at the end, but something we cultivate in our hearts, homes, and relationships now. Imagine the impact that would have on the way we treat one another, the way we navigate conflict, the way we live.

Living in peace means accepting ourselves and others as we are. It means choosing compassion over judgment, connection over division, and calm over chaos. It means letting go of the need to always be right, to always be busy, to always be achieving, and instead, finding contentment in the simple moments of life. Living in peace means being present, being grateful, and being kind, first to ourselves and then to others.

We all deserve to live in peace, not just rest in it. Life is too precious, too fleeting, to spend our days consumed by stress, conflict, or striving for something just beyond our reach. Peace isn't a far-off destination it's a choice we can make every day. So why wait until the end to seek it? Let's find peace now, in how we live, love, and show up in the world. We owe it to ourselves and to each other to live in peace, here and now.

Save your energy

There comes a point in life when you no longer have the energy for meaningless friendships, forced interactions, or unnecessary conversations. As you grow and evolve, you begin to see through the superficiality of many relationships. You recognize when people are not being genuine, when their words are empty, and when their actions don't align with their intentions. It becomes exhausting to engage in shallow exchanges when you know they lack substance and truth.

You begin to realize that not all relationships serve your well-being, and some interactions are simply draining. It's no longer enough to go through the motions of small talk or to maintain friendships out of obligation. When you reach this point, you find yourself craving authenticity real connections with people who understand you, who respect your energy, and who are honest with themselves and you.

Seeing through the lies and facades of others can be disheartening, but it's also liberating. You no longer feel the need to play along or pretend. Instead, you start valuing your time and emotional energy, reserving it for people and experiences that bring true connection and meaning. There's no space for forced smiles or shallow conversations when you can clearly see the difference between truth and pretence.

In this stage of life, you seek depth and authenticity. You choose to surround yourself with individuals who are real, who speak with sincerity, and who contribute to your growth rather than deplete your energy. It's not about closing yourself off but about recognizing that life is too short to waste on interactions that don't nourish your soul.

As you grow more aware, it becomes easier to let go of these meaningless connections. You stop participating in relationships that don't serve you, freeing yourself to focus on what truly matters: building genuine, supportive, and honest connections with people who see you for who you are. This shift allows you to live with more clarity and peace, no longer weighed down by the superficiality of interactions that have lost their value.

Don't absorb, just observe

The ability to understand a situation or a person without becoming overly attached or emotionally entangled allows for greater clarity and open-mindedness. When you can observe the world around you without absorbing the emotions, opinions, or energy of others, you free yourself from unnecessary stress and maintain your own balance.

Often, we tend to absorb the emotions and energies of those around us, especially when we care deeply. We may internalize others' pain, frustration, or anger, taking it on as our own. While empathy is a valuable trait, absorbing too much of what others feel can cloud our judgment and prevent us from seeing situations objectively. When you're constantly soaking up the emotional atmosphere around you, your mind becomes overwhelmed, and it becomes harder to think clearly, make decisions, or act with purpose.

Observing, on the other hand, means you can witness and understand what's happening without letting it overwhelm you. It's about creating a healthy distance between yourself and the situation, allowing you to process things with a clear, unbiased mind. This detachment doesn't mean indifference, it means staying grounded in your own thoughts and emotions while remaining open to understanding different perspectives.

When you practice observing without absorbing, you develop greater emotional resilience. You're able to recognize when someone is upset, angry, or frustrated, but instead of letting their emotions dictate your reaction, you stay centered. This emotional distance allows you to respond thoughtfully rather than react impulsively. You become more open-minded because you're not immediately pulled into the emotional intensity of a situation. Instead, you can step back, consider all sides, and see the bigger picture.

This trait of observing rather than absorbing is key to becoming more open-minded. Open-mindedness requires the ability to look at different perspectives without letting personal biases or emotions cloud your judgment. If you're always absorbing the thoughts and feelings of others, it's easy to get caught up in their narratives and lose sight of your own truth. By practicing observation, you can take in new information, reflect on it, and make decisions based on your values and beliefs, not just on the emotions of the moment.

When you're able to observe and not absorb, you're also better equipped to engage in meaningful conversations and interactions. You can listen to others without feeling the need to agree or adopt their perspective. Instead of becoming defensive or emotionally reactive, you can calmly consider what's being said, weigh its merits, and either incorporate it into your understanding or respectfully disagree. This kind of detachment fosters deeper discussions and encourages the exchange of ideas, promoting growth and learning.

In your relationships, this approach can also help you maintain healthy boundaries. By observing rather than absorbing, you can offer support to those you care about without becoming consumed by their struggles. You maintain your own emotional well-being, which makes you more capable of offering genuine help. When you absorb too much of someone else's pain, it can leave you drained, and neither of you benefits from that dynamic. By observing with compassion, you stay grounded in yourself, offering a more stable, clear-headed presence for those who need you.

This shift in perspective doesn't mean disengaging from life or becoming emotionally detached. Instead, it's about recognising that you have control over what you let into your emotional space. You can witness, understand, and even empathise without carrying the full weight of what you observe. This skill allows you to live with greater peace, clarity, and openness.

Ultimately, "observe, don't absorb" is about fostering a healthy balance between empathy and self-preservation. By observing with understanding and curiosity rather than absorbing and reacting, you allow yourself to stay grounded, maintain your own emotional health, and approach life's challenges with an open, calm, and clear perspective. You become more flexible in your thinking, less reactive, and far more capable of handling whatever life throws your way.

Chapter 17

Lead by example

It is a hard truth to accept, especially when we deeply care about someone. We often want to step in, offer solutions, and make things better for them. We believe that if we just guide them enough, if we offer the right advice or the perfect solution, we can help them change. But the reality is, no matter how much you try, people must choose to change for themselves. You can lead them to the door, but they have to decide to walk through it.

It's natural to want to help, especially when you see someone struggling, making unhealthy choices, or repeating self-destructive patterns. You might think that by giving them the right guidance, you can steer them toward a better path. But real change only happens when the person is ready and willing to make that shift. No matter how well-intentioned your efforts are, true transformation can't be forced from the outside it has to come from within.

People are complex, with layers of experiences, emotions, and beliefs that shape their actions. You can't simply "fix" someone because they are not broken parts to be repaired. Their choices, behaviours, and patterns are deeply tied to their personal journey, and only they can decide when it's time to change course. This realization can be difficult, especially when it feels like you're watching someone make choices that hurt themselves or others. But understanding that they have their own path to walk is important.

When you try to fix someone, you take away their opportunity to grow through their own experiences. Change requires ownership people must take responsibility for their actions and decisions to truly transform. Without this self-driven realization, any change they make will be superficial or temporary, because it wasn't motivated by their own desire to improve.

Think of it like planting a seed. You can provide someone with the tools they need to grow you can offer advice, support, and encouragement but they have to nurture that seed themselves. If they are not ready to do the work, no amount of effort on your part will make it happen. They must water the seed, tend to it, and care for it themselves. You can't force it to grow for them.

Sometimes, your role is simply to be a guiding light. You can point them in the right direction, show them what's possible, and offer them support along the way. But you must also accept that you cannot force someone to change. They must be the ones to take that first step and commit to the process of growth. It's their journey, and only they can walk it.

When you accept this truth, you relieve yourself of the burden of trying to control someone else's path. You stop feeling responsible for their choices and focus on offering support in a way that respects their autonomy. Leading someone toward change is about empowering them to make their own decisions, not about fixing them. You can inspire, encourage, and provide guidance, but ultimately, they must decide to change for themselves.

People need to come to their own conclusions and face their own realizations. Change is often driven by a moment of self-awareness, where they see the need for growth and decide to act. This can't be handed to them, it has to be experienced. Your role is to be patient, offer wisdom when they seek it, and trust that they will come to their own understanding in their own time.

At the heart of this understanding is the realization that you are not responsible for anyone else's growth but your own. You can be a positive influence, but you cannot do the work for someone else. And that's okay. Letting go of the need to fix others doesn't mean you stop caring, it means you respect their ability to make their own choices and take ownership of their life.

The most powerful thing you can do is to lead by example. Show them what's possible by embodying the change you wish to see in them. Live your truth, demonstrate growth in your own life, and trust that they will find their way when they are ready. Change is a deeply personal journey, and the decision to transform is theirs alone.

Be optimistic and believer

Imagine if you invested the same energy you use to doubt yourself into truly believing in who you are and all that you can achieve. What if, instead of focusing on worst-case scenarios, you spent your time envisioning the best possible outcomes? The truth is, we often pour so much energy into self-doubt that we forget how powerful belief can be. But just as we've trained our minds to dwell on the negative, we can retrain our minds to focus on optimism, to embrace hope, and to become our biggest supporters rather than our harshest critics.

Think about how often you second-guess yourself those moments when doubt creeps in, convincing you that you're not good enough, that things won't work out, or that failure is inevitable. That kind of thinking doesn't just drain your energy; it shapes your reality. Doubt becomes a filter through which you see the world, holding you back from opportunities, growth, and the fulfilment of your potential. But imagine flipping that script. Imagine using that same mental energy to build yourself up, to dream big, and to take action toward your goals with confidence. The power to do that lies within you.

It all begins with the way you talk to yourself. If you constantly tell yourself that you're not capable or that things will go wrong, your mind starts to believe it. That's how doubt becomes a habit. But the amazing thing about the mind is that it can be retrained. Just as you've trained yourself to think in patterns of self-doubt, you can guide your mind toward optimism and belief in yourself. It's not about ignoring challenges or pretending everything will always be perfect it's about choosing to focus on the possibilities, the opportunities, and the best-case scenarios.

Start by becoming aware of your thoughts. When you catch yourself spiraling into doubt, pause and ask yourself, "What if the best happens? What if everything works out? What if I'm more capable than I realize?" By simply shifting the direction of your thoughts, you begin to open your mind to new possibilities. You start to create a mindset that's not afraid of failure but excited about potential.

Optimism isn't about being naïve or unrealistic. It's about having faith in yourself and believing that good things can happen. It's about understanding that, while setbacks may come, they don't define your journey. Optimism is the belief that there's always something you can do, some action you can take to move forward. It empowers you to see opportunities in challenges, lessons in failure, and growth in every experience.

When you choose optimism, you're not just hoping for the best you're creating it. Your actions, fuelled by positive belief, lead to better outcomes because you're approaching life from a place of possibility rather than fear. The more you practice believing in yourself, the more natural it becomes. Your mind can be guided, retrained, and reshaped to support you rather than limit you.

You can start right now. Each time doubt creeps in, challenge it. Replace it with thoughts that uplift you. Train yourself to focus on what could go right instead of what might go wrong. Over time, this mindset shift will transform the way you approach life, goals, and even challenges. You'll find yourself more resilient, more confident, and more open to the idea that you're capable of achieving great things.

Optimism isn't about waiting for the perfect moment; it's about making the moment perfect by believing in your ability to handle whatever comes your way. You have the power to choose your mindset, and by choosing optimism, you create a life filled with more hope, more courage, and more success. So, why not start now? Let go of the doubt and invest your energy in belief. Believe in who you are, in all you can do, and in the best-case scenario waiting for you.

People come and go

People come and go, and that's just a natural part of life. We often form deep connections with others, believing or hoping they'll be around forever, but the reality is that most people in our lives are temporary. While this may seem unsettling at first, it's actually a truth that can bring you peace and acceptance. Understanding that people will enter and exit your life at different times allows you to embrace relationships for what they are in the moment, without clinging to them when it's time to let go.

Every person we meet plays a role in our journey, whether it's to teach us something, offer support during a particular phase, or share experiences that shape us. Some people stay for a long time, and others are only with us briefly. The length of their presence doesn't always determine their impact. Even temporary connections can leave a lasting imprint on who we become.

When we accept that people are temporary, we begin to appreciate our time with them more deeply. Instead of focusing on the fear of losing them, we can focus on the value they bring while they're in our lives. This mindset allows us to enjoy relationships for what they are, rather than what we wish they would be. It's about embracing the moments and memories, knowing that not every relationship is meant to last forever and that's okay.

By recognizing that people come and go, you also free yourself from the pain of holding on to relationships that have run their course. Sometimes, we try to force people to stay in our lives out of fear or comfort, but doing so only creates unnecessary strain. Letting go doesn't mean forgetting or devaluing the connection it means understanding that every relationship has its own timeline, and when it's time for someone to leave, it's part of the natural flow of life.

Accepting this truth helps you grow emotionally. It teaches you to cherish the moments and people while they are with you and to be okay when it's time to move on. People enter your life for different reasons, and as you evolve, your relationships will change too. Some friendships and connections will stand the test of time, while others will fade. But each one serves its purpose in shaping who you are.

Life is a series of changing relationships, where the only constant is you. Understanding that most people are temporary allows you to let go with grace and hold on to the memories with gratitude. It helps you live more freely, appreciating every connection while knowing that life continues to flow, bringing new people and experiences into your journey.

Chapter 18

Keep the brain engaged

The brain thrives when it's exposed to new experiences and challenges. Engaging your brain means pushing it beyond its comfort zone, constantly feeding it fresh information, and encouraging it to make new connections. Just as physical exercise strengthens muscles, mental stimulation keeps the brain sharp, adaptable, and capable of growth. When you seek new experiences, whether it's learning a skill, traveling, or engaging in creative activities, you challenge your brain to think in different ways, fostering both intellectual and emotional growth.

New experiences trigger neuroplasticity, which is the brain's ability to rewire itself and form new neural connections. This is how we learn, adapt, and grow throughout life. When you expose your brain to unfamiliar tasks or situations, you stimulate these processes, keeping your mind flexible and resilient. This is why trying new things such as learning a language, picking up a hobby, or engaging in complex problem-solving helps you develop cognitively and emotionally.

A brain that remains stuck in routine becomes complacent. While familiarity can be comforting, it can also lead to stagnation, limiting your capacity for creativity, critical thinking, and adaptability. By seeking out new challenges, you ensure that your brain continues to expand its abilities. New experiences force you to approach problems with fresh perspectives, allowing you to think more creatively and develop solutions you might not have considered otherwise.

In essence, keeping the brain engaged means feeding it a steady diet of novelty, challenge, and variety. The more you seek out new experiences, the more agile and adaptable your brain becomes, equipping you to better navigate both the familiar and the unknown.

Value your own needs

Don't set yourself on fire to keep others warm. Far too often, people sacrifice their own self-respect, value, and well-being to make others comfortable. It's a habit that's easy to fall into, especially for those who are caring or empathic by nature. But over time, this pattern of self-sacrifice can lead to exhaustion, resentment, and the erosion of your own sense of self-worth.

We tend to give too much of ourselves in relationships, friendships, and even at work, without realizing the toll it takes. You may find yourself constantly saying "yes" to requests, even when it stretches you thin. Or perhaps you go out of your way to solve everyone else's problems, neglecting your own needs in the process. You might compromise your values or set aside your boundaries to avoid conflict or make someone else happy. In doing so, you slowly chip away at your own self-respect and personal value.

It's a natural desire to want to help others, to be there for the people you care about. But when you do this at the expense of your own well-being, you end up burning yourself out. You're setting yourself on fire, thinking it will keep others warm, but in reality, you're left depleted and they may not even recognize the sacrifice you've made. Worse, they may start to expect it, taking more and more without realizing the damage it's causing you.

Over time, this can lead to losing sight of your own needs and boundaries. You start to feel like your worth is tied to how much you give to others, how much of yourself you can sacrifice. This is a dangerous place to be because it makes it easy to ignore the signs that you're running on empty. You tell yourself it is fine to put others first, but eventually, this leaves you with nothing left for yourself.

Part of this issue stems from a lack of self-respect or fear of disappointing others. You might fear that saying "no" will make people think less of you, or that setting boundaries will cause conflict. But in reality, by consistently putting others before yourself, you teach people that your needs don't matter. You set a precedent that it's okay for others to take advantage of your time, energy, and generosity. Over time, this not only diminishes your sense of self-worth but can also lead to resentment toward the very people you've been trying to help.

Sacrificing your own well-being for the sake of others creates a cycle of imbalance. You may think you're doing it out of love or responsibility, but in the end, you're sacrificing your own happiness and peace. To break this cycle, it's crucial to recognize when you're giving too much and to start setting boundaries that honour your own needs.

You have the right to say "no" without guilt. You have the right to prioritize your well-being over the expectations of others. And you have the right to stop giving so much of yourself that it leaves you empty.

True generosity comes from a place of balance. When you respect yourself and value your own needs, you can give to others from a place of fullness, not sacrifice. By setting healthy boundaries, you allow yourself to remain whole while still being there for those you care about. It's not selfish to take care of yourself, it is necessary. Because in the end, you can't truly help others if you've already burned yourself out in the process.

Don't wait for the right moment

The more you live like you are already the person you want to become, the faster that vision turns into reality. It's a simple yet powerful idea. Instead of waiting for external factors to align or for some future moment to start living your dreams, you begin embodying the traits and behaviours of your ideal self today. By doing so, you create the momentum that drives you toward that version of yourself faster than if you were to simply wait for change to happen. The more you embrace the actions, mindset, and habits of the person you want to be, the quicker you transform into that person.

This concept isn't about pretending or faking it; it's about making a conscious decision to align your daily actions with the future you envision for yourself. Often, we fall into the trap of thinking we need to wait until we've "made it" to start living like the person we want to become. We think, Once I achieve X, then I'll be the confident, successful, and disciplined person I want to be. But in reality, transformation happens when we begin acting like that person long before we've reached our goals. By taking ownership of who you want to be today, you start shaping your future in a tangible way.

Imagine, for example, that you aspire to be someone with a healthier lifestyle, someone who exercises regularly, eats well, and feels energized. Instead of waiting until you reach a certain weight or fitness level to adopt that identity, you start making choices now that reflect that version of yourself. You choose to exercise today, eat healthier meals, and make decisions that prioritize your health. Over time, these consistent actions compound, and before you know it, you're living the life of the person you've always wanted to be.

The same principle applies to any aspect of life whether you want to be more successful, more confident, more creative, or more disciplined. If you want to be successful, start by acting like the successful person you envision. How would they approach their work? What kind of habits would they have? How would they handle setbacks or challenges? When you start answering these questions and acting accordingly, you set yourself on a fast track to becoming that person. By embodying success today, you're not only training your mind to believe it's possible, but you're also reinforcing behaviours that lead to success.

This is the power of living in alignment with the future you want. Each small action you take in line with that future version of yourself brings you closer to realizing it. When you live like the person you want to become, your brain begins to see it as reality. Instead of thinking, "I'll be successful someday", you start thinking, I am on the path to success now and that shift in mindset is critical.

But living like the person you want to become isn't always easy. It requires discipline, focus, and sometimes discomfort. You'll need to push through old habits, let go of limiting beliefs, and step into a version of yourself that feels new or unfamiliar. This can be challenging, but it's also incredibly rewarding. By pushing through discomfort, you're actively creating change. Every time you make a decision that aligns with your future self, you're building momentum that moves you closer to your goals.

Moreover, this approach to life encourages you to stop waiting for external validation. Often, we wait for others to recognize our potential before we give ourselves permission to act on it. We might think, once my boss notices my hard work, then "I'll step up" or "Once I get that promotion, I'll be more confident". But true transformation happens when you stop waiting for permission and start giving it to yourself. You don't need someone else's approval to start living like the person you want to be. That's a decision only you can make and the sooner you make it, the faster your life will begin to change.

When you start living like your future self today, you're essentially telling the universe (and yourself) that you're ready for the next step. You're showing up in a way that says, I'm prepared for this, and in doing so, you attract the opportunities, people, and circumstances that align with that version of yourself. This is how living in alignment with your future self-accelerates your growth. You're no longer waiting for things to happen to you; you're actively creating the conditions for your transformation.

It's important to remember that this isn't about rushing through life or being inauthentic. Living like the person you want to become means intentionally making choices that are in line with your vision for yourself, but it also means being patient with the process. Change doesn't happen overnight, and there will be setbacks along the way. But the more consistently you act in alignment with your future self, the closer you get to embodying that person in reality.

At its core, this approach is about taking responsibility for your own growth. It's about understanding that the person you want to become isn't some distant figure you'll eventually meet it's someone you can start becoming today, through your actions, your mindset, and your habits. The more you live like that person now, the sooner you'll see the changes reflected in your life.

So, stop waiting for the "right" moment to begin. Start acting like the person you want to be today. Every decision you make in alignment with your future self brings you one step closer to that reality. Live like you're already the version of yourself you aspire to be, and watch as your world transforms to match the future you've been working toward. The sooner you embody the person you want to become, the sooner that vision turns into your reality.

Chapter 19

Embrace silence and be comfortable

The compulsion to fill the silence often reveals something deeper our discomfort with ourselves. Many of us feel the urge to break quiet moments with chatter, as though the silence exposes us in a way we're not ready to confront. By constantly speaking or creating noise, we distract not only others but also ourselves, avoiding the deeper truths that might surface in the quiet.

When silence falls, it's as if the mask we wear starts to slip. The persona we've carefully crafted, the one we present to the world, suddenly feels inadequate in the face of stillness. We fill the silence with words, even if they're unnecessary, because it keeps us from sitting with our own thoughts or emotions. Noise becomes a form of protection, a way to keep up the illusion of who we think we're supposed to be, instead of allowing ourselves to simply be.

This need to fill the silence isn't just about avoiding awkwardness with others it's also about avoiding awkwardness with ourselves. If we are truly comfortable in our own skin, silence doesn't feel threatening. But when we're unsure or insecure, silence can feel like it's calling attention to the cracks in our armour. We fill the gaps with noise because we're afraid of what others might see or worse, what we might discover about ourselves.

By constantly filling the silence, we continue to play a character, a version of ourselves that we think others will find more appealing. We speak out of a need to entertain or to keep the peace, rather than out of genuine expression. In doing so, we drift further away from our authentic selves, using noise as a way to mask the truth of who we are. The irony is that while we may think we're building connection through constant talking, we're often just reinforcing a barrier between who we are and how we present ourselves.

This pattern also keeps us from truly connecting with others. When we fill every silence, we miss the chance to experience the depth that quiet moments can bring. Silence allows for reflection, for the kind of listening that goes beyond words. When we are comfortable with silence, we give both ourselves and others the space to exist authentically, without the pressure of constant performance.

The next time you feel the need to fill a quiet moment, pause and reflect. Ask yourself: Why do I feel the need to speak right now? Am I truly engaging, or am I avoiding something within myself? When we begin to understand that our compulsion to fill silence is rooted in discomfort with ourselves, we can start to embrace those quiet moments. Rather than using noise to appease others or distract ourselves, we can learn to sit comfortably in our own presence, allowing authenticity to surface.

In embracing silence, we not only become more at peace with ourselves but also deepen our connections with those around us. We no longer need to play a role or create distractions. Instead, we can be present, authentic, and comfortable both in silence and in conversation.

Free yourself from criticism

Your idea of me is not my responsibility to live up to. This powerful statement carries a deep message about personal freedom, authenticity, and the weight of others' expectations. It reminds us that the perceptions, opinions, and judgments others hold about us are not ours to carry. We are not obligated to mould ourselves to fit the image someone else has created. Instead, we are tasked with the far more important work of living authentically, in alignment with our own values and truths.

From a young age, we are shaped by the expectations of others, parents, teachers, friends, society at large. These expectations form a mould that we may feel pressured to fit into, and over time, we can start to confuse these external ideas with who we truly are. We start to live in ways that align with what others expect of us, rather than what is true for us. The beliefs and thoughts that others have about who we should be begin to cloud our own sense of identity.

One of the biggest barriers to living freely from others' opinions is the deeply ingrained need for approval. Human beings are social creatures, and it's natural to want to be accepted and validated by others. However, when we tie our sense of worth to external validation, we begin to live for others rather than for ourselves. We prioritize fitting in over standing out, even when doing so requires us to suppress parts of who we are. This approval-seeking mentality can become a prison, limiting our growth, creativity, and authenticity. It's a mindset that says, "I must be what they expect, or I will not be enough."

This need for approval also stems from a fear of rejection or criticism. We may believe that if we don't meet others' expectations, we will be judged, abandoned, or misunderstood. This fear can keep us trapped in cycles of trying to please everyone, often at the expense of our own happiness. But the truth is, no matter what we do, we cannot control how others perceive us. Their opinions are filtered through their own experiences, beliefs, and biases, and they do not reflect our true worth. When we recognize that we cannot please everyone and that it isn't our job to try we begin to free ourselves from the weight of their expectations.

Another belief that can block us from rejecting others' ideas of us is the internalized belief that we owe something to those around us especially those closest to us, like family or friends. There's a sense of obligation to fulfill the roles we've been assigned, whether that's the responsible child, the successful partner, or the agreeable friend. We may feel that stepping outside these roles and living according to our own values would disappoint or hurt the people we care about. However, while others may have certain ideas about who we are, it's important to recognize that their beliefs are shaped by their own experiences and desires, not necessarily by who we truly are or what we need.

True liberation comes when we realize that we are not responsible for maintaining the image others have of us. We are only responsible for being true to ourselves. This means embracing who we are at our core, regardless of how it aligns with the expectations placed upon us. When we begin to let go of the need to live up to others' ideas of us, we reclaim our power to define ourselves.

Living authentically requires courage. It means accepting that some people may not understand or approve of who we are, and that's okay. Their misunderstanding is not our burden to carry. It also means recognizing that we can still love and care for others without needing to fulfill the role they've envisioned for us. In fact, living true to ourselves often deepens our relationships, as it allows for more genuine connection and respect.

At its core, the belief that "your idea of me is not my responsibility to live up to" is about freeing yourself from the confines of others' expectations. It's about recognizing that your value doesn't come from how well you fit into someone else's mould, but from how fully you embrace your own identity. When we let go of the weight of others' opinions, we create space for true growth, fulfilment, and self-acceptance. We begin to live not for others, but for ourselves.

Create space for clarity

If it is out of your hands, don't keep it in your head. We often find ourselves stressed or anxious over things that are beyond our control whether it's the actions of others, unforeseen circumstances, or future outcomes we can't predict. Yet, despite knowing we can't change these external factors, we let them take up space in our minds, creating internal stress that weighs us down. Understanding this dynamic is crucial to finding peace: not everything is meant to be controlled, and learning to let go is essential for mental well-being.

Life is full of uncertainties, and while it's natural to want control, many things are simply outside of our reach. A job outcome, another person's behaviour, or the twists and turns of life are often beyond what we can influence. When we focus on these uncontrollable aspects, we give them more power than they deserve, allowing them to dominate our thoughts. The truth is, holding on to what you can't control only creates unnecessary internal stress and anxiety.

Imagine a situation where you've done everything you can whether it's preparing for a presentation, having a difficult conversation, or applying for a job. At some point, the outcome is out of your hands. No amount of worrying or overthinking will change the result. However, it's easy to keep replaying scenarios in your head, fixating on possible outcomes or what could go wrong. This mental cycle doesn't help it just drains your energy and clouds your focus.

The challenge lies in recognizing when something is beyond your control and choosing to release it. Letting go doesn't mean you're giving up or being passive; it means you're accepting that you've done what you can and that it's time to stop carrying the weight of the unknown. It's about focusing on what you "can" control your reactions, your mindset, and how you move forward.

Holding on to things we can't control doesn't just cause stress it often makes the situation feel bigger and more overwhelming than it really is. The more you dwell on it, the more power you give it. By releasing those thoughts, you free up mental space for clarity, calm, and creativity. You allow yourself to focus on the present moment, where your attention is needed the most.

On the flip side, some internal stress comes from emotions or thoughts we suppress. Instead of addressing them, we let them swirl around in our heads, unresolved. If you find yourself overwhelmed by something within, like a lingering worry or fear, it's important to confront and process it. Sometimes, the act of writing down your thoughts, talking to someone, or practicing mindfulness can help release that internal stress. By addressing the emotions rather than letting them fester, you reduce their hold on you.

Peace comes from realizing that not everything needs to be controlled. Some things are meant to be released from your mind once they're out of your hands. Focus on what you "can" manage your mindset, your actions, your present and let go of the rest. By doing so, you'll create more space for clarity and peace in your life.

Chapter 20

Focus on improving

It is easy to get caught up in the desire to prove yourself to others. Whether it's at work, in social circles, or even with family, we often seek validation, approval, and recognition by showing others our worth. But the truth is, trying to constantly prove yourself can be exhausting and, ultimately, unfulfilling. Instead of pouring energy into proving yourself to others, imagine redirecting that energy toward improving yourself. When you focus on your personal growth, self-awareness, and betterment, the approval you seek often comes naturally as a by-product.

Proving yourself to others usually means living by their standards, trying to fit into their expectations, and chasing external validation. But when you shift your focus toward improving, the change is internal. You're no longer trying to impress anyone; instead, you're striving to become the best version of yourself for your own fulfilment and sense of purpose. When you focus on improvement rather than approval, you build skills, gain confidence, and grow in ways that are more authentic and lasting.

Those who focus on self-improvement understand that validation comes from within. They don't need to constantly seek out others' approval because they trust their own path. Ironically, this mindset shift often leads to the very approval they no longer chase. When you stop trying so hard to prove yourself, others begin to notice your natural growth, strength, and authenticity. It's through this process of self-improvement that people come to recognize your worth without you having to force it upon them.

Improvement is about embracing your own potential, setting personal goals, and working on areas where you can grow. It's about building character, developing resilience, and being open to learning from both successes and failures. As you become more focused on bettering yourself, others see this growth and naturally begin to respect and value you for who you are, not just for what you're trying to prove. True respect comes from showing, not telling.

When you're in a cycle of trying to prove yourself, you give power to others. Your worth becomes tied to how they perceive you, and you become reactive, constantly adjusting to meet their expectations. But when you focus on improvement, you take back that power. You're no longer waiting for others to validate you; you're becoming stronger, wiser, and more confident on your own terms.

It's important to understand that improvement is a lifelong process, and the need to prove yourself fades as you grow. The more you improve, the more you realize that proving yourself to others was never really necessary. People who genuinely care will notice your efforts, your integrity, and your growth and they will respect you for it. Approval will come, not because you sought it, but because you've become someone who deserves it through constant self-betterment.

So, shift your focus. Instead of trying to prove yourself to others, work on improving yourself for yourself. You'll find that as you grow, others will notice and appreciate the progress, without you needing to constantly seek their validation. In the end, it's the journey of self-improvement that matters, and the approval you once sought will naturally follow.

A person is unknown

You don't truly know a person until you've travelled with them, handled money together, experienced their anger, or lived alongside them. While everyday interactions can give you a glimpse into someone's personality, it's in these deeper, more intense situations where their true character emerges. These moments challenge the surface-level niceties and reveal how they handle stress, discomfort, and compromise.

Traveling with someone is one of the quickest ways to get to know their true self. When you travel together, you're placed in unfamiliar environments, often dealing with the unexpected. Delays, missed flights, wrong directions, or tiredness bring out traits that aren't usually visible in daily life. Does the person remain calm and adaptable, or do they get frustrated easily? Do they share the responsibility of planning and decision-making, or do they become passive or controlling? These travel experiences show how someone manages discomfort and how they treat others when under pressure.

Money is another significant factor that can reveal a lot about a person's character. Whether you're splitting bills, managing shared expenses, or dealing with a financial disagreement, how someone handles money often reflects their values and priorities. Are they fair and transparent, or do they become stingy or secretive? Do they take advantage of generosity, or are they uncomfortable discussing finances? Money can create tensions in any relationship, and seeing how someone navigates these situations shows their level of integrity and responsibility. A person's attitude toward money whether they're generous, fair, or manipulative can be a clear indicator of their overall character.

Anger is another emotion that strips away the façade people often maintain. You don't truly know someone until you've seen how they react when they're angry. Everyone gets upset from time to time, but how a person handles their anger is key. Do they lash out, becoming hurtful or destructive, or do they manage their emotions in a calm, controlled manner? Anger reveals a person's emotional intelligence and ability to navigate conflict. It also highlights whether they are respectful, even when frustrated, or if they lose control and damage relationships.

Finally, living with someone reveals the most intimate aspects of their character. Daily life together exposes habits, routines, and responsibilities that are easy to hide in casual settings. You see how they treat shared spaces, how they contribute to household tasks, and how considerate they are of your needs. Living together requires patience, compromise, and communication. Do they pull their weight, or do they leave you to carry the load? Are they respectful of your personal space and time? These small daily behaviours speak volumes about how they will treat you in the long run.

Ultimately, it's in these challenging or intimate moments that the true self comes out. Traveling, managing money, experiencing anger, and living together all force someone to reveal their deeper tendencies. These situations test patience, fairness, and emotional control, and they give you insight into who a person really is beyond their polished exterior. If you want to truly know someone, see how they act when things are difficult, not just when life is easy.

Pushing someone to improve

Encouraging personal growth and development is one of the most profound ways to show you care about someone. It's not about highlighting their flaws or trying to control them; it's about seeing their potential and helping them unlock it so they can experience deeper, more meaningful connections. True love isn't content with stagnation. It wants to see the other person thrive, evolve, and become the best version of themselves.

When we push someone to improve, we are supporting them in cultivating qualities that allow love to flourish such as patience, empathy, self-awareness, and emotional resilience. These qualities not only make them better partners, friends, or family members but also enable them to have a healthier, more fulfilling relationship with themselves. Personal growth helps clear away barriers like insecurity, fear, or emotional baggage that might be holding them back from fully experiencing and expressing love. By encouraging someone to improve, you're empowering them to break through these limitations.

This process of improvement enhances a person's capacity to love. When someone works on themselves whether that means addressing their weaknesses, healing from past traumas, or developing emotional intelligence, they become more open to giving and receiving love. They are more equipped to handle the ups and downs of relationships with grace and understanding, which leads to stronger, more lasting bonds. As people grow, they learn how to better communicate, show vulnerability, and be more compassionate. These are all key elements in building deeper, more authentic connections with others.

It's also important to recognize that pushing someone to improve isn't about perfection or controlling their path. It's about supporting them on their journey toward self-betterment, knowing that this journey is what will allow them to love more fully and freely. Improvement doesn't mean changing who they are; it means helping them become more aligned with their true self the version of themselves that isn't held back by insecurity, fear, or past mistakes. When you encourage someone to improve, you're saying, "I see the best in you, and I want to help you bring that out."

Often, we think of love as accepting someone exactly as they are, and while that is an essential part of loving someone, it doesn't mean we should ignore the areas where they can grow. Real love is about both acceptance and encouragement. It's about loving someone for who they are today while also believing in their potential for tomorrow. Pushing someone to improve isn't rejecting who they are; it's believing in the greatness they're capable of achieving.

In fact, improvement allows people to love themselves more, too. As they grow and overcome challenges, they gain confidence, self-worth, and inner strength. This self-love is crucial because it sets the foundation for all other relationships. Someone who has taken the time to improve their inner world by working through insecurities, building resilience, or developing emotional intelligence is more capable of loving themselves in a healthy way. This self-love then extends outward, allowing them to love others without insecurity, jealousy, or fear holding them back.

It's also worth noting that when someone loves you enough to push you to improve, they are showing deep faith in your potential. They see the best version of you, even when you might not see it yourself. This act of love isn't about criticism; it's about believing that you are capable of so much more. People who push you to improve aren't trying to tear you down; they are investing in your future happiness and success, knowing that personal growth will only enhance your ability to live a more fulfilling, connected life.

Ultimately, pushing someone to improve is one of the most loving things you can do. It's a way of saying, "I believe in you, and I want to support you in becoming the best version of yourself." By encouraging someone to grow, you are helping them experience a fuller capacity to love and be loved. It is an investment in their ability to build stronger relationships, navigate life's challenges, and become someone who can love with greater depth, patience, and understanding.

Chapter 21

Be good to yourself

It is easy to be kind, patient, and forgiving to the people around us, but when it comes to ourselves, we tend to be overly harsh, self-critical, and demanding. What if, instead, you chose to offer yourself the same compassion and understanding you give to those you care about?

Imagine how different your life could be if you were your own best friend. No one understands your experiences better than you. You're the only one who fully knows your struggles, triumphs, insecurities, and dreams. And because of that, you're in the best position to support yourself through life's ups and downs. When you stop being so hard on yourself, you create space for healing, growth, and self-acceptance. You allow yourself to make mistakes, learn, and move forward without carrying the weight of harsh self-judgment.

Being good to yourself is more than just treating yourself to nice things or engaging in self-care routines; it's about changing the way you speak to yourself, how you view your worth, and how you handle setbacks. Often, we talk to ourselves in ways we'd never talk to a friend. We berate ourselves for not being perfect, for making mistakes, or for not achieving goals as quickly as we'd like. But imagine if, instead of criticizing yourself, you offered words of encouragement. What if, when things got tough, you told yourself, "It is okay. I'm doing my best, and that it is enough?"

When you shift your perspective and start treating yourself with kindness and respect, you unlock a whole new level of personal empowerment. The truth is, no one can help you the way you can. While others can offer advice, support, and comfort, ultimately, you are the one who decides how to respond to challenges, how to navigate life's complexities, and how to heal from past wounds. By being kinder to yourself, you strengthen your inner resilience, making it easier to overcome obstacles and bounce back from difficulties.

This doesn't mean you have to be perfect. Self-compassion isn't about pretending everything is always great or ignoring areas for growth. It's about accepting yourself fully, flaws and all, and understanding that you are deserving of love and respect, even from yourself. In fact, especially from yourself. When you treat yourself with kindness, you build a foundation of self-worth that becomes unshakeable, even in the face of adversity.

Life becomes better when you treat yourself better. The more you practice self-kindness, the more you'll notice that things that used to weigh you down feel lighter. Challenges that once seemed overwhelming become manageable because you've cultivated an inner support system. You're no longer battling against yourself but working with yourself, lifting yourself up rather than tearing yourself down.

Remember, being good to yourself isn't selfish, it's essential. You can't pour from an empty cup, and by taking care of yourself, you're also ensuring that you have the energy and capacity to be there for others. So, be your own best friend. Offer yourself the same love and compassion you give to those around you. Your life will be richer.

Try after failing

The power of not giving up cannot be overstated. Every failure is an opportunity to reflect upon your mistakes, understand what went wrong, and learn how to avoid the same pitfalls in the future. This process of reflection and learning is essential for growth and improvement. It transforms failures into valuable lessons, equipping you with the knowledge and experience to tackle challenges more effectively.

For beginners, failure can be daunting. It might feel like a setback or a sign that they are not good enough. However, it's important to understand that failure is a natural part of the journey to mastery. Every master was once a beginner who faced numerous challenges and setbacks. The key difference is that masters see failure not as a defeat but as a stepping stone to success.

By not giving up, you build resilience and develop a mindset that embraces challenges. This persistence helps you push through difficulties and stay focused on your long-term goals. Each time you fail and get back up, you are one step closer to mastery. You gain insights that you wouldn't have discovered otherwise, making you wiser and more capable.

Failing also provides the power to refine your approach. When you fail, you get a clear indication of what doesn't work. This clarity allows you to adjust your strategies and improve your techniques. Over time, these small adjustments accumulate, leading to significant progress and development.

The willingness to persist through failures is what ultimately distinguishes a master from a beginner. Embrace your mistakes, learn from them, and keep moving forward. Remember, every master was once a beginner who refused to give up.

Choose your company wisely

To protect your well-being and long-term success, it's crucial to understand the profound influence others can have on your life. People who consistently display reckless or harmful behaviour are not just a temporary distraction; they can fundamentally impact your decision-making process and lead you down paths that are difficult to recover from.

When you surround yourself with individuals who lack regard for consequences or engage in patterns of instability, it becomes easier for their habits to bleed into your own life. These influences can lead to impulsive decisions that may jeopardize your personal, professional, or even financial stability. Whether it's through peer pressure, adopting similar behaviours, or becoming involved in situations you otherwise would have avoided, the consequences can be far-reaching.

Therefore, a crucial part of safeguarding your progress and achievements is practicing keen observation and sound judgment. Look for clear signs of recklessness or irresponsibility, such as frequent risk-taking without consideration of potential outcomes, a pattern of blaming others for mistakes, or consistently avoiding accountability. These traits are often warning signs that this person may not have your best interests at heart.

Establishing clear boundaries and distancing yourself from these influences is necessary to preserve your hard-earned progress. Boundaries are not a sign of weakness or selfishness but a protective measure to ensure you don't get swept up in harmful patterns. Prioritizing relationships with individuals who share your values, aspirations, and level of responsibility is key. Such people will uplift and motivate you, providing the type of support system that encourages growth rather than hindering it.

Positive relationships act as a stabilizing force, helping you maintain focus and clarity. They offer constructive feedback, which is essential for growth, while also providing emotional and psychological safety. Being surrounded by those who value your well-being and share a similar drive for success makes it easier to stay on track, avoid distractions, and keep your goals in sight.

The company you keep has a profound impact on your ability to thrive. Prioritizing relationships that nurture your ambitions while distancing yourself from those that threaten to derail your progress is a fundamental step in ensuring that your efforts lead to long-term success. By surrounding yourself with people who inspire you to be the best version of yourself, you can continue to flourish and achieve your dreams.

Chapter 22

Navigate relationships and connections

In a world where conversations seem constant, it's easy to mistake superficial interactions for genuine connections. Many people believe they're engaging in meaningful dialogue, but in reality, they're just waiting for their turn to talk. This common mistake leads to confusion between true friendship and shallow exchanges, leaving many feeling unheard, misunderstood, and frustrated.

True friendship involves deep listening, listening not just to respond, but to understand. When someone is truly invested in you, they don't just hear your words; they pay attention to your emotions, your tone, and your underlying needs. They aren't rushing to offer their own opinion or advice. Instead, they're fully present, absorbing what you're saying, and giving you the space to be heard. These are the people who make you feel valued, like your words matter and your thoughts are important.

But the sad reality is, many people don't engage with that level of care. Instead, they're caught in the habit of simply listening to respond. While you speak, they're already formulating their next point, waiting for their chance to jump in and shift the focus back to themselves. This isn't done out of malice, but often out of habit or self-absorption. The result, however, is that conversations feel shallow and unsatisfying because they lack true connection.

This is where the confusion arises. Superficial interactions, where people only listen to speak, not to understand, can easily be mistaken for friendship. Just because someone is there, nodding along or engaging in conversation, doesn't mean they're truly connecting with you. It's easy to mistake these surface-level interactions for support or care, but over time, you'll start to notice the lack of depth.

Genuine relationships require more than just exchanging words. They require the patience and empathy to truly hear what someone is saying. When someone isn't just waiting for their turn to talk, they ask follow-up questions, they dig deeper, and they sit with you in your thoughts. They don't rush to offer advice or divert the conversation. Instead, they create a space where you feel understood, even if they don't have all the answers. This kind of interaction is what builds trust and fosters real friendships.

Recognizing the difference between those who listen to understand and those who listen only to respond is crucial for your emotional well-being. When you find yourself in conversations where the other person is more focused on their own words than yours, it's a sign that the connection may not be as deep as you'd hoped. These interactions often leave you feeling drained or unheard, no matter how long the conversation lasts.

It's important to surround yourself with people who value genuine connection. These are the ones who, instead of waiting for their turn to talk, wait for the right moment to show they understand. They don't just hear you; they see you, and they make sure you feel that your voice matters.

So, as you navigate friendships and connections, keep in mind that not everyone who talks with you is truly engaging with you. Look for those who listen with intention, who aren't just waiting to respond but are genuinely trying to understand. Those are the people who are capable of building real, lasting relationships, ones that go beyond superficial interactions and into the realm of true friendship.

Healers confront pain

Healers are not perfect. They are not untouched by flaws or immune to struggle. In fact, it is through facing their own imperfections and overcoming adversity that they gain the power to heal others. A healer's journey isn't defined by a flawless existence, but by the deep understanding that comes from rising above their own challenges. The beauty of a healer lies in their ability to transform their wounds into wisdom, and it's this transformation that enables them to offer guidance and support to others.

A true healer is someone who has confronted their own pain, fears, and insecurities and has worked to heal those parts of themselves. They have experienced darkness, yet chosen to emerge into the light. This process of healing themselves is what makes them so effective in helping others. They know what it's like to feel lost, broken, or uncertain, and because of that, they can meet others in their own pain with empathy and insight. Healers understand that healing is not a straight line but a continuous journey of growth.

Through adversity, healers are strengthened. They are not born with an inherent ability to heal, they develop it through their experiences. Each hardship, each moment of struggle, shapes them into who they are. It is their resilience, their capacity to grow through pain that defines them. They don't shy away from their own imperfections but work through them, learning more about themselves and the human experience along the way. This makes their work more authentic because they are healing from a place of experience, not theory.

The very imperfections they've healed within themselves are often the areas where they are most effective in helping others. If a healer has struggled with self-worth, they can guide others toward finding theirs. If they've battled through grief, they know how to comfort those in the depths of sorrow. It's not about having all the answers, but about having walked through the fire and coming out the other side with a deeper understanding of what it means to be human.

Healers don't just inspire others with their words, they inspire with their stories. They are living examples of what it means to get better through adversity. Their presence alone serves as a reminder that healing is possible, that progress can be made even when it feels impossible. They inspire not by being perfect but by being real, by showing that imperfection is part of the journey and that healing is a process we all have access to.

Healers show us that we, too, can heal our wounds, that we can face adversity and come out stronger. Their ability to guide others stems from their own healing, their own growth, and their ongoing commitment to becoming better versions of themselves. They remind us that healing is not about achieving perfection but about embracing the process of getting better, both for ourselves and for those we seek to uplift.

So, the next time you think of a healer, don't think of someone without flaws. Think of someone who has healed enough of themselves to offer their hand to others, someone who has found strength in their scars and now uses that strength to help others heal theirs. They are living proof that, through adversity, we can all find our way to a better, stronger version of ourselves.

Respecting your journey

This is a fundamental truth: the people who've succeeded, the ones truly ahead of you, have no interest in tearing you down. They've been through the struggles, the doubts, and the uncertainty. They remember what it felt like to start from the bottom, to push through obstacles and setbacks. Instead of belittling you, they recognize your journey. They'll often encourage, advice, or simply observe, because they respect the process. Success, after all, doesn't breed contempt, it breeds understanding.

But the ones who haven't dared to try? The ones who are stuck in their own fear, their own stagnation, those are the people who will have the most to say. They're the ones who'll criticize your efforts, mock your small beginnings, and doubt your potential. It's not because they see something wrong in you, but because they see something lacking in themselves. Your ambition, your determination, reminds them of what they haven't done, of the risks they were too afraid to take. In their eyes, tearing you down is easier than facing their own fears.

This is where a key realization comes in: the judgment that stings often comes from those who aren't even in the game. They stand on the side-lines, watching but never daring to play, and their words are simply a reflection of their own unfulfilled potential. If you listen too closely to their criticism, it's easy to start doubting yourself, wondering if you're on the right path. But the truth is, their negativity isn't a reflection of your journey, it's a mirror of their own insecurities.

On the flip side, the right people in your life, those who have succeeded in their own paths, will always offer you the truth. Not the harsh, baseless criticism that tears you down, but the kind of truth that helps you grow. A bodybuilder will tell you where your form can improve because they know it's essential for progress. A successful entrepreneur will share their failures and what they learned, guiding you away from similar pitfalls. An NBA player might point out a flaw in your technique, but they do so to make you better, not to mock your efforts.

The right people tell you the truth because they want to see you succeed. They respect your journey, and their honesty is grounded in experience, not judgment. They know that real growth comes from facing hard truths, not from avoiding them. And they understand that support doesn't always mean sugar coating, it means helping you recognize where you can improve, where you can push yourself further.

Surround yourself with those who speak from experience and truth. The ones who are rooting for you, not from a place of insecurity, but from a place of respect and wisdom. Let go of the judgment from those who haven't even started their own race. Remember, it's easy for someone below you to have something to say, but it's the ones who've climbed higher that will offer you the insight and truth that will push you to new heights.

In the end, the right people will always respect your journey. They won't judge your efforts; instead, they'll honour the work you put in, the courage you show, and the progress you make. They'll tell you the truth, not to hurt you, but to help you become the best version of yourself.

Chapter 23

Integrity and alignment

Integrity has no need for rules. When you possess integrity, you naturally act in alignment with what is right, not because you are following rules, but because you understand the purpose behind them. Rules exist to guide behaviour and maintain order, but when someone lives with integrity, their choices are driven by internal values rather than external regulations.

When you fully grasp the "why" behind a rule, it ceases to feel like a restriction. You understand its purpose and, as a result, follow its principles without needing to be told. A person with integrity does the right thing, even when no one is watching, not because they fear punishment or seek reward, but because it is ingrained in who they are. Their actions are rooted in an internal compass that points toward honesty, fairness, and responsibility.

Consider how rules function in society. They are created to ensure people act ethically, maintain order, or protect others. But if everyone acted with integrity, the need for strict rules would diminish. People wouldn't need to be told not to cheat, lie, or harm others because they would already be living by those values naturally.

For example, the rule of treating others with respect is often formally enforced in workplaces or communities. However, someone with integrity doesn't need this rule to be written or enforced to know that treating others with kindness is the right thing to do. They understand the inherent value of respect, so they embody it without thinking twice about whether it's required. This deeper understanding of values allows people with integrity to act appropriately in all situations, even when there are no rules to guide them.

When you live with integrity, you don't see rules as limitations but as reflections of values you already uphold. You act not out of obligation but out of a genuine understanding of what's right. This approach fosters trust and respect, as others can see that your actions are authentic, not driven by fear of consequences.

In essence, integrity allows you to transcend rules. When you fully internalize the reasons behind a rule, you no longer need it to govern your behaviour. Your actions become a natural extension of your values. You act not because you're told to, but because you understand the impact of your choices.

So, remember, integrity isn't about following rules for the sake of it. It's about living in alignment with the principles that guide those rules. When you understand and embrace those principles, rules become unnecessary, you'll already be doing what's right.

Avoid comparison with others

We often look at others and measure our success, happiness, or worth against theirs, without realizing that comparison is an unhelpful behaviour that only creates a sense of disparity between ourselves and the world.

When you compare yourself to someone else, you're looking at only a fraction of their reality. You see the external, the highlight reel, the achievements, or the polished image they present to the world. But you cannot see the depth of who that person truly is. You don't see their struggles, insecurities, or the challenges they face behind the scenes. Yet, we often assume that what we see on the surface is the whole picture, leading us to feel inadequate, as though we're falling behind or missing out.

The truth is, comparison blinds us to our own unique journey. It pulls our attention away from what we've accomplished, the challenges we've overcome, and the person we're becoming. Instead of appreciating our growth, we focus on what we don't have or what we think we're lacking in comparison to others. This mindset breeds dissatisfaction, making it nearly impossible to feel joy in the present moment.

One of the most harmful aspects of comparison is that it encourages a false sense of competition with others. It creates a divide, making it seem like we're all in a race where only one person can win. But life isn't a competition. Everyone has their own path, their own timeline, and their own lessons to learn. By focusing on someone else's journey, you lose sight of your own, which is entirely unique and cannot be compared to anyone else's.

It's essential to understand that what you see in others is not the whole story. You cannot truly know the depth of another person's experiences, struggles, or emotions. Comparing yourself to their outward appearance or successes is like comparing the cover of one book to the pages of another. It's an incomplete view and doesn't account for the full complexity of each person's life.

Instead of letting comparison steal your joy, shift your focus inward. Appreciate your own progress, no matter how small it may seem. Celebrate the steps you've taken toward your goals, the growth you've experienced, and the challenges you've overcome. When you stop measuring your worth against others, you'll find that joy comes more easily, because you're no longer distracted by a false sense of inadequacy.

Remember, the only person you should compare yourself to who you were yesterday. Progress is personal, and your journey is yours alone. When you let go of comparison, you reclaim your joy, allowing yourself to appreciate your own path and the unique value you bring to the world.

Don't seek revenge

The rotten fruit will fall itself, Don't seek revenge. When faced with negativity or harm, the instinct to retaliate often rises, but revenge rarely leads to resolution. In fact, responding to negativity only pulls you into the same destructive energy, wasting your time and peace. The truth is, those who sow discord and harm will eventually face the consequences of their actions. The universe has a way of balancing itself, and rotten fruit, those whose negativity infects everything will fall by their own doing.

The best response to negativity is nothing at all. By refusing to react, you rise above the situation, maintaining your integrity and peace of mind. Silence can be the most powerful response, as it leaves no room for escalation and deprives the negative person of the attention they crave.

In the end, those who thrive on spreading harm will face the natural consequences of their behaviour. Their actions, like rotten fruit, will eventually decay and fall. Rather than seeking revenge, focus on your growth, knowing that time will reveal the truth without you lifting a finger.

Chapter 24

Understanding constructive criticism

Criticism is an unavoidable part of life. Whether it comes from friends, family, co-workers, or even strangers, we all encounter it at some point. However, not all criticism is created equal, and one of the most important lessons you can learn is this: don't take criticism from someone you wouldn't take advice from.

It's easy to let negative feedback affect us, especially when it's harsh or unexpected. But think for a moment about who that criticism is coming from. Would you seek out this person's advice if you were struggling or looking for guidance? If the answer is no, then why give their criticism so much power?

Often, the loudest critics are those who have the least insight into your life or your goals. These individuals may criticize your choices, your work, or your dreams, but their words say more about them than they do about you. People who offer destructive criticism are often projecting their own insecurities or frustrations. Seeing you strive for something or make progress can trigger feelings of inadequacy in them, which leads them to criticize your efforts. This kind of criticism is rarely about helping you improve, it's more about them trying to bring you down to their level.

On the other hand, constructive criticism comes from people who genuinely want to see you grow. These are the individuals whose advice you would seek out because you respect their perspective, experience, and insight. When they offer feedback, it's not to tear you down, but to help you improve. Their criticism, even if hard to hear, comes from a place of support and encouragement. These are the voices that matter because they are invested in your success and personal development.

By learning to distinguish between these two types of criticism, you gain a valuable tool: the ability to filter out negativity that doesn't serve you. The next time someone criticizes you, pause and ask yourself: Would I take this person's advice if I were struggling? If the answer is no, then there's little reason to let their negative opinions affect your confidence or direction. Their words are simply noise, and they don't deserve a place in your thoughts.

This doesn't mean you should ignore all criticism, on the contrary, feedback from trusted sources can be incredibly helpful. It's about being selective with whose criticism you take to heart. People who are living a life you admire, who have walked a path similar to yours, or who genuinely care about your growth are the ones whose opinions you should value.

The more you focus on the right voices, the more empowered you become. You stop letting meaningless criticism shake your confidence and instead stay focused on your goals. In the end, not every voice deserves your attention. By only taking criticism from those whose advice you would trust, you protect your energy, stay true to yourself, and continue on your path to success and personal growth.

So, remember: if you wouldn't take advice from them, don't take their criticism. Focus on the voices that truly matter.

Be harder to manipulate

Set boundaries to be hard to manipulate. It's easy to feel like the problem when you begin to recognize patterns of manipulation in your life. You might find yourself pulling away from certain people, setting boundaries, and even cutting ties with those you once trusted. However, these decisions can often be labelled as selfish, especially by those who benefited from your previous lack of awareness. But here's the truth: recognizing manipulation isn't selfish, it's a sign of growth and wisdom.

When someone manipulates you, they often twist the narrative to make you believe you're at fault. They create situations where you're always the one to blame, where you're expected to bend, adjust, and sacrifice for their benefit. Slowly, you might start internalizing their perspective, wondering if you're too demanding, too sensitive, or simply difficult. And when you begin to push back, you may even feel guilty, questioning whether you're the one in the wrong.

This is a common tactic used by manipulators, they make you doubt your instincts. They rely on your empathy, your desire to maintain relationships, and your willingness to please others. The moment you step back and assert your needs, they may accuse you of being selfish. But here's the empowering truth: this isn't selfishness. It's self-awareness.

Realizing you're being manipulated doesn't mean you're hard to get along with or incapable of maintaining relationships. It means you've learned to spot unhealthy dynamics and are taking action to protect yourself. These realizations might be difficult at first because they force you to confront uncomfortable truths about the people around you. But they also give you the power to reshape your life and prioritize relationships that are healthy, supportive, and mutually beneficial.

Feeling selfish for distancing yourself from a manipulative person is natural, but that feeling often stems from how deeply ingrained the manipulative behaviour has become in the relationship. You've been conditioned to feel responsible for their emotions, their well-being, and their happiness. So when you decide to break free from that cycle, it's jarring, not just for them, but for you, too. You may second-guess your actions, wondering if you've become too harsh, too closed off. But that couldn't be further from the truth.

In reality, your awareness of manipulation shows strength and growth. You're learning to honour your needs, set healthy boundaries, and invest your time and energy into people who genuinely care about you. This awareness doesn't mean you've stopped caring about others; it means you've started caring about yourself, too.

Instead of feeling guilt or shame for protecting your peace, realize this: you're choosing to spend your time wisely. You're no longer available to those who drain your energy, exploit your kindness, or take advantage of your willingness to compromise. You're no longer the person who says "yes" just to avoid conflict. You've grown wiser, and that's something to celebrate, not criticize.

As you become more selective with your time and energy, you might notice a shift in your relationships. The people who are genuinely supportive of you will respect your boundaries, while those who thrived on manipulation may try to guilt-trip or shame you. But remember, their discomfort is not your responsibility. They're reacting to the fact that they can no longer control you, and that's a reflection of them, not you.

In the end, you're not selfish for realizing you've been manipulated. You're wise. You've learned a crucial lesson about who deserves your time and attention. You've grown, and with that growth comes the freedom to cultivate relationships that uplift, rather than drain, you.

So the next time you're called selfish for protecting your peace, take it as a sign that you've evolved. You're no longer willing to play a role in someone else's narrative at the expense of your own well-being. That's not selfishness, that's self-respect. And in a world that often tries to make us feel small for standing up for ourselves, self-respect is one of the most empowering things you can possess.

Accepting people

Accepting people as they are is an important part of life, but that doesn't mean they should have unlimited access to your time, energy, or space. Just as a CEO manages their company, you must manage your life by placing people where they belong. Each person you encounter is responsible for their own growth, their own choices, and their own direction. Your job is not to fix or guide them, but to understand where they fit in your life while maintaining the boundaries that honour your well-being.

People must help themselves if they want to grow or change. You cannot carry the weight of someone else's journey on your shoulders, nor should you feel obligated to. Everyone has their own path, and while you can offer support and compassion, you can't do the work for them. At some point, each person must decide which direction they want to take. And it's up to you, as the CEO of your life, to recognize this and act accordingly.

Not everyone belongs in the same position in your life. Some people are meant to be close, involved in your inner circle, while others may need to be kept at a distance. This isn't about judgment, it's about recognizing what's best for your mental and emotional health. Setting boundaries doesn't mean you love or care for people any less; it simply means you respect yourself enough to decide who and what influences your life.

Having boundaries doesn't just protect your energy; it also allows others to take responsibility for their own actions. When you accept people as they are but place them where they belong, you're encouraging them to own their journey. You're letting them know that while you accept and care for them, they must be accountable for their own choices and growth.

This process requires a deep respect for both yourself and others. You respect yourself by setting clear boundaries that protect your peace and allow you to thrive. And you respect others by letting them navigate their own lives without trying to control or rescue them. When you approach life this way, you empower yourself and those around you to live authentically and independently.

Ultimately, it's about balance. You can accept people as they are without letting their choices disrupt your life. You can offer support while maintaining boundaries that keep you grounded. And, as the CEO of your life, you decide who gets to play a close role and who may need to step back. It's not selfish, it's an act of self-respect, one that helps you create a life that aligns with your values, energy, and goals.

By accepting people as they are and placing them where they belong, you allow both yourself and others the freedom to grow. You lead your life with purpose, understanding that each person is responsible for their own journey while ensuring that your own well-being remains intact.

Chapter 25

Reflection of thoughts

The world is a reflection of what we think. No one is truly bothering you, everything you experience comes from how you perceive the world around you. What if, for a moment, you consider that the struggles you feel with others, the frustrations, the conflicts, are not with the outside world but within yourself? This might seem hard to accept at first, but the truth is, we all experience life through our own unique lens. The world we see is shaped by our thoughts, emotions, and past experiences. We are not simply reacting to reality; we are creating our own reality based on what we believe.

When you understand that your thoughts colour everything around you, you begin to realize that the battles you think you're having with others are often battles with yourself. That person who irritates you, the situation that feels unfair, the things that make you anxious or upset, they are not inherently bothersome in themselves. Instead, your reaction to them is what creates the discomfort. You are fighting with your expectations, your beliefs, and your interpretations. What you see as a problem is often just a reflection of unresolved feelings or limiting thoughts within you.

This doesn't mean that the world is perfect or that difficult situations don't exist. Life is full of challenges. But how you experience and respond to those challenges is entirely within your control. If you believe the world is unfair, you will see unfairness everywhere. If you believe people are out to hurt you, you will interpret their actions through that lens. On the other hand, if you believe the world is full of opportunities and growth, even in the face of hardship, that's what you'll find.

This is why taking accountability for everything in your life is so crucial. It's not about blaming yourself for things that have happened to you but about recognizing that you have power over how you experience and respond to life. Accountability is freeing because it puts you back in control. When you stop blaming others or external circumstances for your unhappiness, you realize that you have the power to change how you think, how you react, and how you approach the world.

Consider this: if your experience of the world is shaped by your thoughts, then changing the way you think can transform your reality. When you take full responsibility for your life, you stop being a victim of circumstance. You understand that your happiness, your peace, and your fulfilment are all within your control, and no one else has the power to take that from you unless you let them.

This is not to dismiss the real difficulties life throws at us. But even in the face of hardship, how we perceive and interpret those challenges makes all the difference. You can choose to see setbacks as failures, or you can choose to see them as opportunities to learn and grow. You can choose to hold onto resentment and anger, or you can choose to let go and find peace within yourself.

When you take accountability, you also take back the power to shape your own life. You realize that while you can't control everything that happens to you, you can always control how you respond. And that is the key to true freedom and inner peace. The more you accept this truth, the more empowered you become to change your life for the better.

Life is not happening to you; it is happening through you. The world reflects your thoughts, beliefs, and perceptions. By understanding this, you have the power to shift your perspective and, in doing so, create a life that aligns with the best version of yourself. Taking responsibility for everything in your life is not a burden, it is the gateway to personal freedom and growth. The moment you fully accept this truth is the moment you become unstoppable in your journey toward peace, happiness, and fulfilment.

Let go of anger

Anger is within you. It is not caused by what someone else says or does, nor by the circumstances you face. It is caused by how you choose to react internally. This might be hard to accept at first, but the truth is that all discomfort, frustration, and pain you feel doesn't originate outside of you, it comes from within. No one can truly affect you unless you allow them to.

When someone says something hurtful or acts in a way that you find upsetting, the anger that rises up is a reaction that belongs to you, not them. It's your internal response to a situation, shaped by your thoughts, emotions, and beliefs. The person or situation might be a trigger, but they do not have the power to create your anger. Only you do.

Imagine how freeing it would be to realize that no one controls your emotions but you. That feeling of discomfort or irritation doesn't come from the outside world, but from how you interpret and process it internally. This doesn't mean that life is free of challenges or that people never act unkindly, it means that you have the power to decide how much those challenges or unkind acts affect your inner peace.

Discomfort, whether it's anger, anxiety, or sadness, is often a sign that something within you is unsettled. Instead of blaming others for how you feel, ask yourself why you're reacting this way. What thoughts are you holding onto that are feeding your anger? What beliefs about yourself or the world are causing you to feel threatened or disrespected? This inner dialogue is the key to understanding that the discomfort you feel is coming from you, not from them.

The moment you realize this, you gain power. Power to change your response. Power to let go of things that don't serve you. Power to protect your peace. No one can make you feel anything without your consent. You choose how much weight to give someone's words or actions. You choose how to interpret your environment. If you find yourself in a state of anger or frustration, it's because you have given those external things permission to disturb your inner peace.

This doesn't mean that you should suppress your emotions or pretend things don't bother you. It means you acknowledge that your emotions are your responsibility. You can feel angry, but you don't have to let it control you. You can be upset, but you don't have to let that upset fester and affect your mental well-being. You have the choice to feel it, understand it, and then let it go.

Imagine the power you would have if you lived life fully aware that nothing can disturb you unless you let it. You'd be unshakable. Situations that used to make you upset would no longer have the same hold over you. People who once triggered you would lose their ability to get under your skin. The world would still be the same, but your inner world would be calm, centered, and in control.

The only person who can control how you feel is "you". Anger, frustration, discomfort, these emotions are within you, and because they are within you, you have the ability to change how you respond to them. This is the ultimate freedom. You have the power to decide how you engage with life. No one affects you unless you allow them to.

By taking ownership of your emotional state, you free yourself from the grip of external forces. You step into a place of strength where you no longer react impulsively to things around you, but instead, respond mindfully from a place of calm. The discomfort you feel is not something others give to you, it is something you create within yourself. And just as easily, you can choose to let it go.

Remember: anger and discomfort are within you, and because they are yours, you have the power to release them. No one has control over you unless you give it to them. Embrace that truth, and you will begin to experience life on your own terms, unburdened by the actions or opinions of others.

Live with harmony

We are meant to live in harmony with our surroundings, not reject them completely. At our core, we are interconnected with the world around us, our environment, the people we encounter, the natural rhythms of life. When we resist or reject our surroundings, we create a sense of isolation and disharmony that affects not only our mental and emotional well-being but our ability to thrive.

Rejecting our surroundings often comes from a desire to control, to shield ourselves from discomfort or from things we don't fully understand. We distance ourselves from situations, people, or environments that we deem undesirable, thinking that by doing so, we can create a sense of safety. But in reality, this resistance creates friction, both within us and with the world around us. Life becomes a struggle against what is, rather than an acceptance of how we fit within the greater whole.

When we are out of harmony with our surroundings, we lose touch with the natural flow of life. We miss the subtle cues, the lessons, and the beauty that comes from being in sync with the world as it unfolds. This disconnection can lead to feelings of dissatisfaction, anxiety, or loneliness, as if we are constantly pushing against life rather than moving with it.

On the other hand, when we embrace our surroundings, when we find harmony with the present moment, with the people around us, and with the environment, we open ourselves up to a deeper sense of peace. Harmony doesn't mean accepting everything without question or staying in situations that harm us, but it does mean recognizing that everything in our life, even the challenges, plays a part in our growth. Instead of resisting, we learn to flow with life's changes, understanding that we are part of something larger than ourselves.

Harmony with our surroundings allows us to be present and engaged with what life has to offer. It means taking time to appreciate the world as it is, not as we wish it to be. By doing this, we connect with the rhythm of nature, the energy of our communities, and the simplicity of everyday experiences. This connection fosters a sense of belonging and purpose, reminding us that we are not separate from the world but a vital part of it.

Finding harmony also involves being attuned to our inner selves. Just as we must respect the environment and people around us, we must also respect our own needs, feelings, and desires. This balance, between ourselves and the world is where true harmony lies. It's about recognizing that life isn't something to be fought against or controlled, but something to be embraced with openness and understanding.

In the end, rejecting our surroundings cuts us off from the fullness of life. To live fully, we must engage with the world around us, finding ways to align ourselves with its natural flow. When we live in harmony with our surroundings, we begin to see that we are not separate from nature, from others, or from life itself. We are part of the whole, and it's in embracing that connection that we find true peace and fulfilment.

Chapter 26

Don't tolerate disrespect

Being too friendly invites a lot of disrespect. This statement, at first glance, may seem harsh or counterintuitive, especially when we are often taught that kindness and friendliness are virtues that foster positive relationships. And while that's true, there's a fine line between being genuinely kind and allowing others to take advantage of that kindness. When you're too friendly, especially without setting boundaries, you may unknowingly open the door for others to treat you with disrespect.

The key issue is not friendliness itself, but the lack of balance between friendliness and assertiveness. Being friendly is a great quality, it shows warmth, openness, and approachability. It can make people feel comfortable and welcome in your presence. However, if you're friendly to the point where you avoid conflict, constantly try to please everyone, or never stand up for yourself, some people may begin to view that as weakness. Over time, this can lead to situations where others take advantage of your good nature or fail to respect your time, feelings, or boundaries.

When you're always trying to be the nice person, constantly putting others' needs ahead of your own, you might unintentionally send the message that your needs are less important. People may begin to assume that you'll always accommodate them, that you'll never say no, or that you'll tolerate behaviours that you're not comfortable with. This doesn't happen because you're not deserving of respect, but because you haven't made it clear that you expect it.

Unfortunately, some individuals will mistake constant friendliness for a lack of self-respect or assertiveness. They may push boundaries, ignore your opinions, or take your kindness for granted. Over time, this can lead to feelings of frustration and resentment, as you start to realize that you're not being treated in the way you deserve. But the fault doesn't lie solely with those who take advantage of your friendliness, it also lies in the absence of clear boundaries.

Setting boundaries is essential in all relationships, whether personal or professional. You can be kind and approachable while also making it clear that you expect others to treat you with respect. Boundaries aren't barriers, they're guidelines that help others understand how you wish to be treated. When you assert your needs in a friendly but firm manner, you show that while you're open and generous, you also value yourself enough to require respect from others.

It's important to remember that respect doesn't come from being intimidating or unfriendly, it comes from mutual understanding. When you set clear boundaries, you're teaching others how to treat you. It's not about being harsh or shutting people out; it's about communicating your needs clearly and assertively. For example, saying "no" when necessary, or speaking up when something makes you uncomfortable, doesn't make you unfriendly, it makes you self-respecting. And people tend to respect those who respect themselves.

In fact, people are more likely to value your kindness when they know it comes from a place of strength rather than an attempt to avoid conflict. When you demonstrate that you can be both friendly and assertive, people will see that you are someone who deserves their respect, not just their affection. You'll be able to build stronger, healthier relationships where your kindness is appreciated and your boundaries are respected.

Another aspect of this balance is learning that not everyone deserves your constant friendliness. Some people will try to exploit your good nature, and it's important to recognize when certain relationships or interactions aren't serving you. You don't have to be friendly to everyone, especially if their behaviour is consistently disrespectful or harmful. Knowing when to step back, distance yourself, or enforce firmer boundaries is a sign of emotional maturity and self-worth.

At the end of the day, being too friendly isn't the problem, it's the lack of boundaries that often accompanies it. You can be a warm, generous person without inviting disrespect, but it requires a balance between kindness and assertiveness. By setting clear expectations for how you want to be treated, you ensure that your friendliness is valued, not taken for granted.

True friendliness comes with self-respect. When you respect yourself enough to expect the same from others, you create relationships that are based on mutual respect and genuine connection. So, while friendliness is a wonderful trait, it's most powerful when paired with the confidence to assert your needs and protect your own well-being. That balance is what ensures that your kindness remains a strength, not a weakness.

Be a well-rounded person

A well-rounded man is an artist, a warrior, and a philosopher a balance of creativity, strength, and wisdom. These qualities, when cultivated together, create a life of depth, resilience, and meaning. Imagine yourself embodying these traits: the ability to express your emotions and ideas, the strength to face challenges head-on, and the wisdom to navigate life's complexities with insight and purpose. To live this way is to live a life of fullness, where both your inner and outer worlds are nurtured and explored.

As an artist, you cultivate your creativity and imagination. This doesn't mean you need to be a painter or musician it means embracing the creative force that exists within you, using it to see the world in new ways and express your inner thoughts. Art is more than a form of expression; it's a way of interpreting the world. Being an artist allows you to explore different perspectives, appreciate beauty in its many forms, and express your emotions in a way that feels authentic and powerful.

Creativity can be found in your approach to problem-solving, in how you navigate relationships, and in the way you pursue your passions. When you cultivate the artist within, you learn to embrace vulnerability, seeing it as a source of strength rather than weakness. Creativity teaches you to think beyond the obvious, to approach life with curiosity and an open heart. It helps you understand that the world isn't black and white there are infinite shades of colour waiting to be explored.

But being well-rounded also requires strength, which is where the warrior comes in. As a warrior, you embody courage, resilience, and discipline. Life will inevitably present challenges some small, some monumental and the warrior within you gives you the strength to face them with determination. This doesn't mean living a life of aggression, but rather a life of conviction and honour.

A warrior is not defined by brute force but by inner strength. It's about having the courage to stand up for what you believe in, even when it's difficult. It's about persevering through life's struggles and showing up, again and again, despite setbacks. The warrior understands the value of discipline, knowing that it takes consistent effort and focus to achieve lasting success. It's about pushing through discomfort in pursuit of growth, understanding that true strength comes not from avoiding challenges but from facing them head-on.

Finally, to be a well-rounded man, you must also be a philosopher a seeker of wisdom. While the artist and warrior help you navigate life's emotional and physical challenges, the philosopher within you asks the deeper questions: "Why am I here? What is my purpose? How do I live a meaningful life?" A philosopher reflects deeply on the world, seeking not just knowledge but understanding.

The philosopher doesn't accept things at face value but is constantly curious, always learning and evolving. This aspect of you helps you make sense of life's complexities and gives you the wisdom to make choices with intention and thoughtfulness. It helps you stay grounded when life feels chaotic, guiding you to seek clarity and meaning even in the most difficult times.

When you combine these three aspects, artist, warrior, and philosopher, you create a life that is rich with balance, strength, and insight. You become someone who is not just surviving but thriving, someone who faces life with passion, resilience, and wisdom. This is what it means to be well-rounded: not to excel in one area alone, but to develop all sides of yourself, embracing both your vulnerability and your strength, your creativity and your logic, your passion and your reflection.

The beauty of cultivating these qualities is that they feed each other. The artist brings creativity to the philosopher's deep questions; the warrior brings strength and discipline to the artist's creative pursuits; the philosopher brings wisdom and reflection to the warrior's battles. Together, they create a powerful, balanced way of living that allows you to face life's joys and hardships with grace, strength, and understanding.

To live as an artist, a warrior, and a philosopher is to live fully. It's about showing up in the world as your authentic self, embracing the complexities of life with courage, creativity, and wisdom. This balanced approach allows you to not only face challenges but to grow from them, turning every experience into an opportunity for deeper understanding and strength. So, step into this way of being. Embrace your creative side, strengthen your inner warrior, and never stop seeking wisdom. The more you cultivate these aspects of yourself, the more well-rounded and fulfilled you'll become.

Stand for reason

True authenticity is rooted in a sense of inner security, independent of external validation. This kind of authenticity means having the strength to stand by your principles, even if it means standing alone. It's about unwavering commitment to your beliefs, showing that true strength comes from within.

Resilience is another key aspect of authenticity. When faced with setbacks, authentic individuals don't stay down; they bounce back stronger. This resilience is what sets them apart, allowing them to grow and develop continuously.

Over time, the steadfastness in maintaining one's true self leads to remarkable personal growth and strength. Authentic individuals, who stay true to their values despite challenges, often find themselves achieving greater heights and stability in their lives.

True authenticity is not just about enduring difficulties but thriving because of them. This inner security and resilience are essential for a fulfilling personal and professional life. As you stay committed to your authentic self, you pave the way for long-term growth and success, surpassing those who rely solely on external factors for their sense of worth.

Chapter 27

Recognise intentions

Some people will pretend to care for you, but their actions and intentions don't reflect genuine love or respect. It's a reminder that not everyone who shows affection truly has your best interests at heart. This isn't about being paranoid or overly suspicious, but about recognizing the importance of understanding someone's true intentions.

At times, it can be difficult to differentiate between those who genuinely care and those who only act like they do. Words can be misleading, and gestures of affection can sometimes hide deeper motives. People may say they love you, but love without true liking or respect is hollow. They may enjoy the idea of having you around, but that doesn't mean they appreciate or value who you are as a person.

This disconnect can happen for a number of reasons. Some people might seek validation, attention, or control. They might find comfort in being associated with you or enjoy the benefits of your presence in their life. But when the relationship is tested, when things get hard or uncomfortable, their true feelings become apparent. If they don't genuinely care, they'll withdraw, leaving you wondering if their affection was ever real to begin with.

This is why understanding the intentions of the people in your life is so crucial. It's not enough for someone to say they love you or shower you with compliments. Do their actions align with their words? Are they consistent in showing up for you, especially when things aren't easy or convenient for them? Love without real respect and liking can feel like an empty performance, leaving you feeling drained and confused.

It's important to ask yourself some hard questions about the people in your life: Are they there for you when it matters, or only when it benefits them? Do they make you feel seen, respected, and valued, or do they simply enjoy the perks of your companionship? You deserve relationships where you don't have to question someone's commitment, where love is rooted in deep, mutual respect, not in superficial appearances or selfish motives.

Taking a step back to assess someone's intentions is a form of self-protection and self-care. It helps you avoid getting caught in emotionally damaging situations where you are giving more than you receive, or where you are staying in relationships that don't honour your worth.

The truth is, love without real connection or respect is not love at all. It's a mask, a façade that can ultimately hurt more than it helps. Genuine love and friendship come from people who don't just act like they love you, but who truly like, respect, and cherish who you are.

When you start to understand and recognize intentions, you empower yourself. You learn to surround yourself with people who are authentic, who lift you up, and who care for you deeply and sincerely. Life is too short to settle for anything less than that. Trust your instincts, and remember that you deserve relationships built on trust, respect, and mutual care, anything less is simply not worth your time.

Mutual Relationships

Your partner is supposed to be your safe place, a haven where you can find comfort, understanding, and support in a world filled with challenges and uncertainties. Relationships are not meant to be another battle in your life; they should be a refuge where you can feel at ease, knowing you are loved for who you are, without judgment or fear. When we enter relationships, we seek a bond that brings a sense of security and peace, not one that adds to the existing chaos and conflict life already throws at us.

Life is tough enough. We all face pressures from work, personal struggles, financial stresses, and the ups and downs of everyday existence. These challenges are inevitable, and they test our strength and resilience. Amidst all this, your relationship should be a source of relief, a place where you can recharge and find balance. The role of a partner is to help ease the burdens of life, not add to them. They are the person you turn to when the world feels overwhelming, the one who offers you solace when you need it most.

But what happens when your relationship becomes a source of conflict? When instead of finding peace, you find yourself embroiled in constant arguments or emotional tension? This is a sign that something crucial is missing. Your partner should never make you feel like you're constantly walking on eggshells, bracing yourself for the next battle. Instead, they should be the one who brings calm to your life, who stands beside you as a teammate, not an adversary.

It's important to recognize that relationships are not about perfection. There will be disagreements, misunderstandings, and moments of frustration. But at the core, your relationship should be built on mutual respect, trust, and emotional safety. When those fundamental pillars are strong, even disagreements can be handled with care, without turning into all-out wars. You should feel secure in the knowledge that your partner values your well-being and will always prioritize your emotional safety, even during challenging times.

If you find yourself in a relationship that feels more like a battlefield than a sanctuary, it's time to reflect on what is truly being nurtured between you. Are you constantly defending yourself, feeling criticized, or emotionally drained? Does every conversation turn into an argument, leaving you more exhausted than supported? These are signs that your relationship is not functioning as the safe space it's meant to be.

In a healthy relationship, both partners work together to protect each other's emotional peace. They understand that life already presents enough challenges, and the relationship should be a place of rest, not additional conflict. Both people should be committed to creating an environment where they can openly share their thoughts, vulnerabilities, and dreams without fear of judgment or attack. When this emotional safety exists, the relationship becomes a source of strength that enhances both partners' lives.

A loving relationship doesn't avoid problems, it faces them with care and empathy. But when the dynamic shifts and the relationship itself becomes the problem, it can feel like yet another battle you're forced to fight. That's not what a partnership is meant to be. You should never have to fight for your peace within your own relationship. Your partner should offer you the reassurance that no matter what happens outside, within the relationship, you are safe.

If you realize that your relationship is no longer a source of comfort, you owe it to yourself to address it. This might mean having difficult conversations, seeking ways to rebuild the emotional safety that has been lost, or, in some cases, deciding that it's time to let go of a relationship that is only bringing you pain. Remember, you deserve a relationship where you feel supported, respected, and cherished, not one that constantly drains you.

Ultimately, your partner is supposed to be your safe place, not another battle in your life. They should be the person who helps you navigate life's difficulties with love, compassion, and support. A relationship grounded in mutual care and respect is one that brings peace, not conflict. If your relationship feels more like a war zone than a sanctuary, it's time to re-evaluate whether it's truly serving your emotional well-being.

Choose calm over conflict

There's no need to fuel conflict when relationships shift. Whether in friendships, partnerships, or otherwise, not all endings require explosive fights or deep-rooted resentment. When respect is lost, it doesn't need to lead to hatred or theatrics; it's simply about recognizing that things have changed and moving forward with grace.

Hate is a heavy burden. It drains energy, demands attention, and traps us in cycles of bitterness that are hard to break. But the fading of respect doesn't have to follow that path. It's not about holding onto anger but understanding that the person or situation no longer holds the same place it once did in your life. And in that awareness, there is no need for hostility.

We often feel pressured to respond dramatically when we lose respect for someone. We're conditioned to think that such changes in relationships require conflict or resentment to validate our feelings. But the truth is, those emotions aren't necessary. You don't need to make the situation bigger than it is. Losing respect is a personal, internal shift, a boundary that's been crossed. It's a recognition that you no longer feel aligned with the person, and that understanding doesn't have to become a spectacle.

There is a quiet power in stepping away without anger, without confrontation, and without the need for a dramatic exit. Letting go of respect doesn't mean you have to shout your feelings from the rooftops or create a scene. Sometimes, the most mature response is to simply acknowledge the shift, accept it, and silently move on. In doing so, you honor your boundaries without creating further tension or chaos.

In a world that often glorifies drama, it can feel unnatural to walk away quietly. But escalating the situation only drains you more. By choosing peace over drama, you protect your energy, safeguard your well-being, and reflect emotional maturity. It's a way of maintaining your dignity while honouring the reality that some relationships change and fade over time.

Not every shift in relationships requires a dramatic conclusion. You don't have to hate someone to let them go. You don't need to fuel conflict to validate your feelings. Losing respect is enough. It's a signal that it's time to redirect your energy toward healthier connections and more fulfilling endeavours.

So, when respect is gone, choose calm over conflict. Choose clarity over chaos. There's no need to create a bigger story than what's already there. Let it be, and let yourself move forward in peace.

Chapter 28

Be kind

Kindness is not a weakness, nor is it something that others should assume will come without boundaries. In fact, the strongest people are those who choose to be kind, knowing full well the impact and consequences of being unkind. They understand that kindness is a choice made from a place of strength, not from a need to please others or to avoid conflict.

Choosing kindness means knowing your worth and respecting others without letting them walk over you. There's a quiet power in being compassionate without allowing yourself to be disrespected or taken advantage of. When you are kind from a place of inner strength, you are saying to the world, "I value myself and others, but I also know where my boundaries are." True kindness doesn't mean saying yes to everything or accepting bad behaviour, it means offering warmth and understanding, while still standing firm in your own values.

The strongest people are those who have experienced the harshness of the world and still choose to respond with kindness. They know the pain that unkindness can cause, both to others and to themselves. They choose kindness not because it's easy, but because they understand its transformative power. It takes strength to remain soft in a world that can be hard, and that strength comes from knowing who you are and what you deserve.

However, kindness doesn't mean tolerating crap. It doesn't mean allowing others to mistreat you, disrespect you, or take advantage of your generosity. When you set boundaries, you protect the value of your kindness. You teach others that while you may offer compassion and understanding, you will not allow your kindness to be exploited.

It's okay to say no. It's okay to assert your boundaries and walk away from situations or people who do not respect them. Your kindness is not for those who abuse it, and your softness is not a license for others to treat you poorly. In fact, being kind while maintaining your boundaries is one of the strongest acts of self-respect you can practice.

So, be kind. Be soft. But never tolerate being taken for granted. The world needs more people who understand the true power of kindness, those who know that real strength lies in choosing to uplift others without sacrificing their own dignity. By protecting your energy, setting boundaries, and standing firm in your worth, you not only honour yourself but also show the world that kindness is not to be mistaken for weakness. It is a conscious, powerful choice that requires both strength and grace.

Your attention is an asset

We invest our attention in things we believe matter. It's a simple truth, yet one that carries incredible weight in how we experience life. Our attention is the currency of our mental and emotional world, shaping the way we think, feel, and engage with everything around us. But here's the challenge: we often give our attention to things that don't serve us, particularly to negativity. Whether it's a toxic relationship, a constant stream of bad news, or internal criticism, we can find ourselves trapped in patterns that drain our energy. And the misconception many of us carry is that these things somehow deserve our focus. The reality is that not everything warrants your precious attention, especially things that only bring negativity into your life.

Your attention is the most valuable asset you have. It's your power to shape the direction of your thoughts, emotions, and actions. Wherever you choose to invest it, you're actively creating your reality. This is why it's essential to recognize that giving attention to things that perpetuate negativity, whether that's a bad habit, unhealthy relationships, or negative thoughts, only reinforces and magnifies those things. What we focus on grows, and if we're not careful, we end up nurturing negativity and inviting it further into our lives.

Consider the way we get caught up in negativity. We might pay attention to what someone said that hurt us, replaying it over and over in our minds. Or we focus on a small inconvenience and let it ruin our entire day. We scroll through social media, comparing ourselves to others, feeling less than, or we immerse ourselves in endless streams of bad news. In each of these scenarios, we are investing our valuable attention in things that deplete us, making them more significant in our lives than they need to be.

It's important to understand that paying attention to negativity is a choice. And while it may feel automatic at times, we always have the power to redirect our focus. The more we feed negative thoughts or situations with our attention, the more power they have over us. We lose our sense of control, our peace, and our ability to cultivate the kind of life we truly want. On the other hand, when we become mindful of where our attention goes, we regain our power.

The things that truly matter, the things that bring you joy, peace, and fulfilment, deserve the bulk of your attention. These are the moments of connection, creativity, learning, and growth. They are the small, beautiful moments that too often go unnoticed because we're too focused on the wrong things. When you learn to give your attention to what uplifts you, what supports your growth, and what nurtures your well-being, you shift your entire experience of life.

By intentionally choosing where to place your attention, you become more aware of what truly deserves your energy. Not every person, situation, or problem is worth your time. The more you focus on negativity, the more it expands in your mind, creating a cycle of stress, frustration, and dissatisfaction. But when you consciously redirect your attention toward positivity, gratitude, and what aligns with your values, your mental and emotional state changes. You feel more in control, more centered, and more at peace with the world around you.

It's not that you need to ignore negative situations entirely, life will always present challenges. But by recognizing the value of your attention, you can decide how much power to give those challenges. You don't have to let them consume you. You have the ability to focus on finding solutions, on learning from difficulties, and on moving forward rather than staying stuck in the problem.

So, the next time you find yourself caught in negativity, ask yourself: "Is this worth my attention?" If the answer is no, consciously choose to redirect your focus. Shift it toward something that serves your well-being that brings you peace or joy. Your attention is precious, and by safeguarding it, you protect your energy, your mindset, and your overall happiness.

Ultimately, your attention is your greatest asset. It's the key to creating the life you want. Be mindful of where you invest it, because where your attention goes, your energy flows. Choose wisely, and watch how your life transforms when you begin to focus on what truly matters.

Self-betrayal

Self-betrayal is putting somebody else's feelings before your own boundaries, but prioritizing yourself is the key to reclaiming your personal power. Prioritizing yourself doesn't mean you're being selfish; it means you're honouring your boundaries and taking care of your own well-being. Boundaries are not about shutting people out, they're about protecting your energy and focusing on what serves your best interests. When you prioritize yourself by using boundaries, you're making a statement that your needs and feelings matter just as much as anyone else's.

Boundaries are the framework through which you define what is acceptable in your life. They're a way of protecting your emotional and mental health, ensuring that you're not overextending yourself or giving to others in ways that leave you feeling drained. By setting and maintaining boundaries, you're creating a safe space where you can thrive, recharge, and engage with others from a place of strength, not depletion.

Prioritizing yourself through boundaries is not about neglecting others; it's about ensuring you have the capacity to take care of yourself first, so you can show up fully in all areas of your life. You're not being selfish, you're being wise. You're choosing to align with what serves your best interests, which in turn allows you to be more present and authentic in your relationships. When you respect your own limits, you're modelling that respect for others as well.

The idea of boundaries can often be misunderstood. It's easy to feel guilty for putting yourself first, but consider this: by prioritizing your needs, you are preserving the best version of yourself. You can't pour from an empty cup. When you honour your own boundaries, you're not just protecting yourself from being taken advantage of you're ensuring that you can continue to grow, heal, and live in alignment with your true self. And when you're thriving, you're in a much better position to support others.

Boundaries are a powerful way of making sure you stay connected to what matters most. They help you filter out what doesn't serve you, whether it's negative energy, unhealthy relationships, or obligations that drain you. This isn't about being self-centered; it's about creating a life that reflects your values, needs, and emotional well-being.

So, when you prioritize yourself, you're not acting out of selfishness. You're showing deep respect for yourself and ensuring that you are living in a way that protects your peace and nurtures your soul. You're choosing to focus on what serves your best interests, which is the foundation of living a balanced, healthy, and fulfilling life.

By setting clear boundaries, you're not just protecting yourself, you're creating space for the things that truly matter to you. You're making room for growth, for joy, and for the relationships and experiences that align with your highest self. So, remember: prioritizing yourself is an act of self-respect. It's about creating a life where your needs, your boundaries, and your well-being come first, ensuring that you can engage with the world from a place of wholeness and peace.

Chapter 29

Find happiness

People who shine from within don't need the spotlight. True happiness isn't something we need to chase outside of ourselves, it's something that already exists within us. In a world that constantly tells us to seek validation through external achievements, recognition, or the approval of others, it's easy to get caught up in the idea that happiness lies in the spotlight. But the truth is, real fulfilment comes from within.

Those who truly shine are the ones who have cultivated an inner peace and confidence that doesn't rely on outside validation. They don't need to be the center of attention, because they understand that their value isn't determined by how much recognition they receive. Instead, they focus on nurturing their own sense of self-worth, knowing that true happiness is something they create internally.

When you rely on external factors, praise, success, material things for happiness, you are putting your joy in the hands of things that are temporary and beyond your control. The highs and lows of life can leave you feeling ungrounded if your sense of self is tied to them. But when your happiness comes from within, it's steady and constant, because it's rooted in who you are, not what you achieve.

Internal happiness is built by doing the inner work: reflecting on your values, understanding your worth, and practicing gratitude for the present moment. It's about cultivating kindness toward yourself, acknowledging your strengths and weaknesses, and finding peace in the everyday moments. When you shine from within, you don't need validation from the outside world to feel good about yourself, you radiate confidence and contentment from a deeper place.

The beauty of this internal glow is that it's not fleeting. It's not something that can be taken away by circumstances or other people's opinions. When you shine from within, you are grounded in your own truth, and that kind of happiness can't be dimmed by external challenges. This inner glow is what makes others drawn to you, not because you're seeking attention, but because you're living authentically.

True happiness is found by embracing who you are and nurturing that connection to yourself. It's not about chasing the next big thing or relying on external praise. The more you focus on building a life that reflects your internal values, the more you'll realize that the spotlight isn't necessary. Your worth doesn't come from how others see you, it comes from how you see yourself.

So, remember, happiness isn't found in the spotlight; it's found in the quiet, internal work of knowing and accepting who you are. The brighter you shine from within, the less you need the external world to tell you how valuable you are. You carry that light with you, always.

Stop being overwhelmed

Rather than viewing these feelings as something to push away, they can be seen as invitations to explore what's happening beneath the surface of our thoughts and emotions. When we take the time to listen to these signals, we start to uncover truths about ourselves, our lives, and the beliefs that shape our experiences.

At its core, feeling down is usually an indication of a misalignment in our internal world. Whether it's a belief about ourselves, a situation, or how we relate to others, negative emotions often point to something we either believe to be true or not true. Perhaps you're feeling inadequate, unworthy, or unsupported, these feelings don't arise randomly. They stem from beliefs that you've either consciously or unconsciously accepted as reality. Your mind and body are reacting to these beliefs, trying to signal that something needs your attention.

In these moments of discomfort, it's easy to want to escape or ignore what's happening inside. But instead of running from the feeling, what if you viewed it as an opportunity for growth? When you allow yourself to sit with these feelings and examine them without judgment, you can begin to uncover the beliefs that are causing the emotional turbulence. By asking yourself questions like, "What belief is driving this feeling?" or "Is this belief really true?" you start to peel back the layers of emotion to get to the root of the issue.

There is immense power in this process. Finding the answers to your own questions is where your true strength lies. Often, we spend so much time looking for solutions outside of ourselves, hoping that someone else can provide the answers or fix what's wrong. But the truth is, the answers are within you. The more you dive into the recesses of your mind and explore the beliefs you hold, the more clarity you'll find. The process of uncovering these truths takes time, and it can be uncomfortable, but it's also incredibly rewarding.

This power of self-reflection is transformative. When you engage in this kind of introspection, you're not just addressing the current emotional discomfort; you're equipping yourself with the tools to handle future challenges more effectively. You'll start to notice that the more you work through these deeper issues, the stronger and more resilient you become. Your power and vitality will slowly begin to grow as you confront limiting beliefs, challenge false narratives, and replace them with more empowering truths.

The process of growth isn't about rushing through the discomfort to feel better quickly. It's about fully engaging with the emotions, understanding their source, and allowing that understanding to guide you toward change. As you begin to explore your inner world, you'll start to build a healthier relationship with your emotions, understanding them as valuable tools rather than obstacles to happiness.

Moreover, as you begin to integrate these insights into your life, you'll notice that the feelings of being down don't last as long or have as much power over you. Instead of seeing these emotions as a sign of weakness or failure, you'll come to recognize them as stepping stones toward a stronger, more authentic version of yourself. You'll discover that your emotional landscape becomes easier to navigate, and the lows no longer seem as daunting because you've learned how to process them in a healthy way.

It's important to remember that feeling down isn't a sign that something is wrong with you. In fact, it's often a sign that you're on the verge of a breakthrough. You're being called to look deeper, to examine the beliefs that are shaping your reality, and to challenge the ones that no longer serve you. The more you engage with this process, the more you'll grow, both emotionally and mentally.

So, when you feel overwhelmed or down, don't see it as a setback. Instead, embrace it as an opportunity to learn more about yourself and to transform the way you think and feel. The power lies within your ability to navigate these emotions, uncover the deeper truths inside you, and ultimately, emerge stronger and more in tune with who you truly are. By choosing to explore your inner world, you are stepping into a path of self-awareness and growth that will lead you to a place of greater peace, vitality, and empowerment.

Choose energy givers

Energy givers only give without expecting anything in return. They uplift you, fill you with positivity, and support your growth without draining your energy. Whether it's a person, activity, or environment, energy givers leave you feeling recharged, centered, and more aligned with your true self. On the other hand, energy takers operate differently. They may give you a temporary boost or hit of energy, but ultimately, they take more from you than they give. Over time, engaging with energy takers leaves you feeling depleted, drained, and emotionally exhausted.

When you make a habit, or even fall into the pattern of addiction, of indulging in energy takers, it becomes a cycle of seeking quick fixes for your energy but constantly ending up feeling worse. Energy takers may appear as friends, toxic environments, unhealthy habits, or even certain mindsets that give you a brief rush of excitement or validation. But once that fades, you're left feeling empty, and the cycle starts again. It becomes harder to break free from their grip because they create a dependence on external validation or temporary satisfaction.

The key to overcoming this struggle is to shift your focus entirely toward energy givers. When you build a habit of surrounding yourself with people and activities that genuinely nourish you, the pull of energy takers weakens. The more you immerse yourself in things that give without taking, whether it's practicing self-care, spending time with uplifting people, or engaging in hobbies that fuel your passion, the more you start to realize how much better you feel when your energy isn't constantly being drained.

Making energy givers a priority creates an internal shift. You begin to feel more empowered, more in control of your own energy, and less susceptible to the temptations of quick fixes that leave you drained. By consistently choosing energy givers, you not only protect yourself from the draining effects of energy takers, but you also strengthen your own ability to recharge and manage your energy effectively. You stop seeking external sources to fill your cup and instead, find fulfilment and balance through sources that genuinely support your well-being.

Eventually, you'll notice that indulging in energy givers makes you less interested in, or even immune to the lure of energy takers. The more you experience the sustained peace and fulfilment that energy givers provide, the less appealing the temporary highs and inevitable lows of energy takers become. You break the cycle of dependency, and instead of feeling constantly drained, you feel continuously uplifted.

Choose energy givers. Make them your habit, your priority, and your source of strength. In doing so, you free yourself from the struggles and emotional fatigue that come with engaging with energy takers. The more you invest in what truly nourishes your soul, the more balanced, fulfilled, and energized you'll feel in all aspects of your life.

Chapter 30

Trust in the journey

It doesn't matter what your goals are, they could be as big as starting a business or as simple as finding more peace in your everyday life. Whether you're striving for something monumental or something that feels more personal, the truth is that your future self has already achieved those things. They've navigated the challenges, overcome the obstacles, and are now living the life you're working toward. The powerful part about this idea is that your future self is not some distant, unreachable version of you, they are an extension of the person you are today.

The goals you have don't need to fit into anyone else's definition of success. They don't have to be ground breaking, life-changing, or even outwardly impressive. Whether you want to become healthier, more confident, better at a hobby, or more fulfilled in your relationships, your future self has already done it. That future version of you exists, and they're a reminder that your dreams are valid, no matter how big or small they are.

What if you could meet this future version of yourself? Imagine putting yourself in their shoes, standing tall as someone who has achieved everything you're aiming for. What advice would they give you? They'd likely tell you to stay patient and consistent, to keep believing in yourself, and to know that setbacks are part of the process. After all, they've already been through what you're facing now. Developing a relationship with your future self allows you to tap into that wisdom and gain a new perspective on your journey. This isn't just wishful thinking, it's an empowering mindset shift.

When you think about your future self, it doesn't matter whether your goals are to build a successful career, form healthier habits, deepen your relationships, or simply feel more content in life. That future version of you is already living those realities. They remind you that every small step you take now is creating the path toward your goals. The relationship you cultivate with your future self helps you stay focused on what truly matters to you.

Having this mindset also helps you avoid the trap of comparison. In a world where we are constantly bombarded with other people's definitions of success, it can be easy to feel like your goals aren't "big enough" or that you should be aiming for something more. But your future self isn't concerned with anyone else's journey. They only care about what matters to you. Whether your dream is to get in better shape, find more time for yourself, or build meaningful connections, your future self has already made it happen and they're proof that you can, too.

No goal is too small or too big to be valid. The important thing is that they are your goals. Every day you spend working toward them, no matter how slow or difficult it may feel, is a step toward the life you want. Your future self is there to remind you that your journey is worth it. They've done the work and know that every challenge you face today will become part of your success story.

So whenever you feel stuck or unsure of the path ahead, remember that the person you want to be is already within you. The future you has achieved everything you dream of, whether those dreams are simple, personal, ambitious, or bold. Trust in the journey, knowing that your future self is waiting, cheering you on, and celebrating each small step you take toward becoming them. They are living proof that you can, and will, achieve the life you're working toward no matter what those goals are.

Accepting criticism and compliments

Life, much like the journey of a growing flower, requires both sunshine and rain. To flourish, we need to embrace the balance between moments of praise and moments of constructive feedback. Compliments and criticism are the two forces that work together to shape us into our fullest potential. They may feel vastly different, but they are equally necessary for our growth. Once you come to accept both with an open heart, you'll realize that every piece of feedback whether positive or challenging can be a stepping stone toward becoming the best version of yourself.

Compliments are the sunshine in your life. They warm your spirit, remind you of your strengths, and give you the energy to keep moving forward. When someone offers you a compliment, they're acknowledging the effort, talent, or kindness they see in you. It's their way of saying, "You're doing great, keep going." In those moments, allow yourself to fully receive the praise. Don't brush it off or minimize it. Take it in, because you deserve it. Every compliment is a small reminder that your hard work, dedication, and unique qualities are being seen by the world. It's like a burst of sunlight, encouraging you to continue along your path.

But just like a flower can't grow with sunshine alone, neither can we. Growth also comes from the rain, the constructive criticism that challenges us to evolve. Criticism might feel uncomfortable at times, and it's natural to want to resist it. But if you shift your perspective, you'll find that criticism can be a gift. It's an opportunity to reflect, adjust, and come back even stronger. Criticism is not meant to tear you down; rather, it's a tool that helps you see where there's room for improvement, where you can push yourself to reach even higher levels of success. It's a reminder that you're not done growing yet, that there's always more to learn, more to achieve, and more ways to refine your skills and character.

Think of a time when you received constructive feedback. Maybe it stung a little at first, but looking back, did it help you grow? Did it make you better in some way? Most likely, it did. The rain may seem harsh, but it nourishes the soil, allowing the roots to grow deeper and the flower to grow stronger. Embrace criticism with an open mind and a willingness to learn, knowing that it's helping to shape you into a more resilient, capable, and well-rounded individual.

When you learn to accept both compliments and criticism with grace, you unlock the power to truly thrive. Compliments give you confidence, reminding you of what you're doing right, while criticism keeps you humble and pushes you to improve. This balance is where true growth happens. It's where you find the strength to keep going, even when things are difficult, and the motivation to continue striving for more.

Imagine yourself as a flower, growing and evolving with each passing season. Sometimes the sun shines brightly on you, filling you with warmth and light. Other times, the rain falls, challenging you to adapt and grow through adversity. Both are necessary, both are beautiful, and both are helping you become the most vibrant version of yourself.

You have a future ahead of you that's full of potential. Every compliment you receive is a signpost along the way, encouraging you to keep going. Every piece of criticism is a nudge in the right direction, helping you adjust course and stay on track toward your goals. Don't shy away from either. Embrace the sunshine and the rain, knowing that they are both essential to your journey.

There will be days when the compliments are few, and the criticism feels overwhelming. On those days, remind yourself that growth takes time. Even the most beautiful flowers don't bloom overnight. They take their time, enduring both the sun and the rain, trusting the process. And just like them, you too will bloom in your own time. The key is to keep going, to keep accepting the lessons life offers, and to trust that every experience is helping you grow.

You are capable of so much more than you realize. With every compliment, let yourself shine a little brighter. With every criticism, let yourself grow a little stronger. Both are working together to help you become the person you're meant to be. So keep going, keep growing, and remember: you are both the sunshine and the rain, and together, they are helping you bloom.

Reality of life

Life is a journey filled with unexpected twists and turns. Along the way, we encounter people and experiences that shape us, teach us, and sometimes, challenge us to our core. But what happens when those people drift away or those experiences don't turn out as we hoped? It's natural to feel a sense of loss, to cling to what could have been, but holding on too tightly to the past keeps you from embracing the future. The truth is, acceptance is the key to moving on, and in moving on, you open yourself up to the endless possibilities that life has waiting for you.

Acceptance doesn't mean giving up or resigning yourself to disappointment. It means making peace with the fact that not everything is meant to stay, and not every chapter is meant to last forever. People change, situations evolve, and sometimes the plans we made for ourselves fall apart. But that's okay. By accepting these truths, you free yourself from the weight of resistance. You allow yourself to heal, to grow, and to make room for new opportunities.

Moving on is not about forgetting or pretending that the past didn't matter. It's about understanding that life is always moving forward, whether we choose to or not. And the sooner we let go of what no longer serves us, the sooner we can step into the new possibilities that await. There's beauty in the unknown. You never know what life can bring you once you release the things that are holding you back.

Consider this: what if, by holding on to the past, you're closing yourself off from something even better? What if, by accepting what has ended, you create space for something far more aligned with who you are now? Life has a way of surprising us when we least expect it, but those surprises can only come when we are open to receiving them.

Ask yourself: "What am I holding on to that is keeping me from moving forward?" Maybe it's a past relationship, a missed opportunity, or a dream that didn't unfold the way you imagined.

Whatever it is, understand that clinging to it doesn't change the past, but it does affect your future. The energy you invest in the past is energy that could be directed toward new beginnings, new experiences, and new growth.

By choosing to accept what has happened, you take back your power. You reclaim your ability to shape your future, rather than letting your past define you. Acceptance is not a sign of weakness; it's a sign of strength. It shows that you trust the flow of life, that you understand there are greater things ahead, and that you are ready to move toward them.

Remember, life has a way of unfolding in ways we can't predict. What you may see as a setback could very well be the thing that leads you to something extraordinary. Moving on isn't about leaving everything behind; it's about making space for what's to come. You never know what life will bring you when you stop holding on to what was and start embracing what could be.

So, let go with grace. Accept the lessons, the memories, and the experiences, but don't let them anchor you in place. Trust that something new and beautiful is on its way, and by moving on, you are walking toward it with open arms. The future holds possibilities beyond what you can imagine, but you must be willing to move forward to see them. Life goes on, and so should you, toward brighter, better, and more fulfilling things.

Chapter 31

True clarity

True clarity begins not with what we see in the world but with what we find within ourselves. When we look out into the world, we find a landscape full of possibilities, a field of dreams shaped by our desires and hopes. Yet, dreams are often scattered, driven by fleeting passions and endless "what ifs." They give us direction, yes, but they also shift and sway with the winds of change, leaving us searching, longing, chasing something we can never quite catch.

But when we turn our gaze inward, something deeper stirs. Inside, we find an anchor, a steady, constant truth. In the quiet spaces of our own heart lies an awakening, a clarity that cannot be touched by external circumstances. This inner landscape is where the real journey unfolds, where our essence resides, waiting to be discovered. To look within is to see beyond illusions and to connect with a part of ourselves that knows who we are, beyond titles, roles, and societal definitions.

Inward reflection brings us face-to-face with both our strength and vulnerability, our dreams and fears. It asks us to confront the unfiltered truth of who we are and to embrace it. This process is not always easy, as it requires us to set aside the distractions of the outside world and listen deeply. But in that stillness, we awaken to a vision of life that is grounded in authenticity and purpose.

This journey into the heart is a call to awaken. It's a reminder that the answers we seek are not "out there" in the shifting sands of external validation, but within, where true wisdom and resilience lie. To look within is to find a path that is yours alone, one that aligns with the deepest parts of your being. Here, you awaken to a vision that guides you, not just through the highs and lows but through the essence of who you are.

"True vision isn't about seeing the world more clearly; it's about understanding yourself more deeply.

Emotions are visitors

Treating emotions like visitors that are just passing through invites us into a profound acceptance of life as it is, without the need to resist, cling, or judge every experience. When we adopt this perspective, we begin to see that emotions, like waves in the ocean, come and go naturally. They rise and fall, sometimes powerfully, sometimes quietly, but they're never permanent. By accepting this ebb and flow, we're reminded of a deeper truth.

Emotions have a way of gripping us, pulling us into their intensity and often making us feel as though they'll last forever. In moments of happiness, we might feel a fear that it will disappear; in moments of sadness, it's easy to believe that the darkness won't lift. This attachment to "good" emotions and aversion to "bad" ones often brings an inner struggle, leaving us feeling trapped in a cycle of seeking one and avoiding the other. But when we start to see emotions as temporary visitors, we gain a sense of freedom from this cycle. Instead of fighting to hold onto joy or banish sadness, we allow them to flow naturally, realizing that their impermanence is a core part of their nature.

Viewing emotions as passing guests can also relieve us of the pressure to make sense of everything we feel. Sometimes, we try to analyse or rationalize our emotions, searching for reasons and solutions as though understanding them fully would allow us to control them. Yet, emotions aren't always logical or easily understood; they don't always have clear sources or fixes. By accepting that things are that way, we let go of the need to explain every feeling and simply allow ourselves to feel. This shift in perspective frees us from overthinking and brings a quiet, liberating peace.

This mindset is about observing emotions without judgment, seeing them as just another part of our human experience. Think of the mind as a clear sky, and emotions as clouds that drift across it. They come in all shapes, sizes, and colours, some heavy with rain, others light and fluffy. But no matter how stormy or bright they may be, they pass in their own time, and the sky, the essence of who we are, remains. The clouds don't alter the sky's existence; they only temporarily affect its appearance. This metaphor reminds us that our true selves remain unchanged, no matter how intense our emotions may be.

In embracing this approach, we develop a more compassionate relationship with ourselves. Rather than feeling disappointed when we experience "negative" emotions or trying to cling to "positive" ones, we learn to hold all feelings with equal respect. Sadness, joy, anger, and peace each have their own rhythms and purposes. Happiness might help us appreciate life's beauty, sadness may deepen our empathy, and anger might signal boundaries that need attention. But none of these emotions are meant to be permanent fixtures; they're simply visitors offering insights and experiences as they pass through.

Accepting that things "just are" doesn't mean we become indifferent or suppress what we feel. On the contrary, it invites us to experience emotions more fully, to allow them to be present without resistance or clinging. Instead of fearing emotions like sadness or anxiety, we can sit with them, acknowledge them, and trust that they will move on in their own time. By observing emotions in this way, we build emotional resilience, knowing that we can face even the most challenging feelings without being overwhelmed.

When we stop trying to control or shape every experience, we're left with a clearer, quieter sense of self. Emotions no longer define us or our worth, and they no longer have the power to destabilize us. We begin to understand that every experience, every feeling, contributes to the larger tapestry of our lives without needing to be held onto or fixed. The practice of seeing emotions as visitors gives us the freedom to approach life with openness, trusting that each moment has something to offer, even if it doesn't come with perfect clarity or comfort.

This perspective also extends beyond emotions to the broader aspects of life. Events, relationships, and experiences all have their own cycles of beginning and ending. By allowing them to unfold without demanding a specific outcome, we start to see that life itself is a flow of moments, each one precious and fleeting. Accepting that things just *are* frees us from trying to control or force our journey. We find peace in the natural flow, knowing that every experience is temporary and that, just like emotions, it will pass when it's ready.

In the end, treating emotions as visitors reminds us of a simple yet profound truth: life is always moving, evolving, and unfolding as it's meant to. Instead of resisting, we learn to trust this process, allowing ourselves to feel, to let go, and to welcome each moment as it comes. This acceptance grants us a deeper sense of freedom, one where we no longer fear the waves of emotion but rather allow them to enrich our journey, trusting in the beauty of things just as they are.

Avoid arguments

Not everyone is capable of considering alternate viewpoints, and recognizing this can save you a lot of unnecessary frustration and conflict. Mental maturity is more than just being smart or experienced, it's the ability to step outside your own viewpoint and genuinely understand where someone else is coming from, even if it challenges your own beliefs.

There are people who, no matter how logically or respectfully you present an argument, are simply not equipped to consider a perspective that doesn't align with their own. They may be locked into their worldview, unwilling to budge or entertain the possibility that there could be another way of seeing things. This is not just stubbornness; it's often a sign of immaturity. Being open to other perspectives requires a certain level of self-awareness and emotional intelligence, qualities that not everyone has developed.

Arguing with someone who lacks this maturity can be like speaking different languages. No matter how much you explain or how valid your points may be, they will only see things from their narrow point of view. It's not because they're trying to be difficult, but because they are mentally stuck. They can't yet comprehend that different perspectives aren't threats, they're opportunities to learn, grow, and expand their understanding of the world.

Real maturity is recognizing that not everyone thinks like you, and that's okay. It's about understanding that you can't force someone to be open-minded. Some people need more time to develop the ability to step outside their own mindset, and that's not something you can change through debate or argument. When you realize this, you gain the power to choose your battles wisely. You no longer feel the need to convince someone who isn't ready to listen, because you understand that it's not about winning an argument, it's about engaging with people who are willing to have a meaningful exchange of ideas.

By pausing to assess someone's mental maturity before diving into an argument, you can save yourself from unnecessary stress and frustration. Some arguments aren't worth having, especially when the other person is more concerned with defending their own position than learning something new. You deserve to engage in conversations that are enriching and open-minded, not ones that drain your energy and leave you feeling unheard.

So, the next time you feel the urge to argue, ask yourself: Is this person truly open to a different perspective, or are they stuck in their own? If they're not ready for a meaningful conversation, it's a sign of immaturity, not of yours, but of theirs. You can choose to walk away, understanding that sometimes, the most mature thing you can do is to not argue at all.

Chapter 32

People change

Things end, people change, and life goes on. These simple truths can feel heavy when we're in the midst of loss, change, or uncertainty. The things we thought were permanent, the relationships, the jobs, the routines can shift or disappear, leaving us feeling disoriented, or even heartbroken. It's easy to feel stuck in the moment, as if the world has stopped because of what we've lost. But even when it's hard to see, life does go on, and with it comes the opportunity for growth, renewal, and new beginnings.

Acknowledging that things have passed can be painful. It's difficult to let go of people who were once close to us, situations that felt familiar, or times when life seemed more certain. But holding onto the past keeps us from embracing the possibilities of the future. Clinging to what was prevents us from seeing the beauty in what could be. While change often feels like loss, it's also an invitation to something new, something better aligned with where we are now.

It's natural to grieve when things end. Change can stir up emotions, sadness, fear, confusion because it disrupts what we know. But even as we grieve, it's important to remember that endings are also beginnings. The space created by change, by the end of one chapter, is an open door to something new. And though it may not be clear what that something new, looks like right now, trust that life is always moving forward, pulling you toward the next step in your journey.

People change, and that includes you. As you grow and evolve, so too do your needs, desires, and dreams. The relationships and situations that served you at one point may no longer align with who you're becoming. And while this can be hard to accept, it's also a sign of progress. Change is a necessary part of growth. It's a reminder that life is fluid, always shifting to accommodate the new version of you that is emerging.

But in the midst of all this change, there is hope. Just because something has ended doesn't mean your story is over. In fact, it may be just beginning. The endings you experience are not roadblocks but rather redirections, guiding you toward new opportunities, new connections, and new paths that you might never have considered otherwise.

Have faith in this process. Life is not static, and neither are you. Trust that the universe is working with you, not against you. What may seem like a loss today can open doors to abundance and growth tomorrow. Sometimes the things we lose are making space for something greater, something that aligns more deeply with who we are becoming.

It's important to embrace the idea that expecting good things, even in the face of change, brings them closer. When you approach life with an open heart, believing that something better is on its way, you create space for prosperity and joy to flow into your life. This isn't about blind optimism, but about recognizing that life is full of seasons, some of loss, yes, but also of renewal, growth, and beauty. Expecting good things, even when you're in a difficult moment, is an act of faith in yourself, in life, and in the future.

So, acknowledge the things that have passed. Let yourself feel the loss, but don't let it keep you from moving forward. Change is a part of life, and it's through change that we find new opportunities to grow, to love, and to experience the richness of life. Life will go on, and so will you, stronger, wiser, and more open to the beautiful possibilities that lie ahead. With each ending comes the promise of something new, and by holding onto that hope, you invite the best into your life.

Trust that life is unfolding exactly as it should. Keep faith in yourself and in the future. What is waiting for you may be more beautiful and fulfilling than anything you've left behind.

Take time to heal

"If you don't heal what hurt you, you'll bleed on people who didn't cut you." This powerful statement speaks to a truth that many of us may not realize: the pain we carry, if left unresolved, can spill into the lives of others, often those closest to us. The wounds we suppress, the emotions we push down, and the traumas we refuse to face can manifest in ways that affect the people who had nothing to do with causing that hurt. It's not because we want to hurt others, but because we haven't taken the time to heal ourselves.

Imagine carrying around unresolved pain, whether it's from past relationships, betrayals, disappointments, or personal failures. That pain doesn't just stay locked away. It leaks into your daily interactions, your moods, and how you show up in relationships. You may find yourself overreacting to small things, feeling distant from those you care about, or projecting your own fears and anxieties onto people who love you and want the best for you. This is the "bleeding" that happens when we don't heal. It's not intentional, but it's a by-product of unaddressed wounds.

But the truth is, people don't deserve to carry the weight of what they didn't cause. The people who love you, who stand by your side, didn't create the hurt, and they shouldn't have to feel the effects of it. Yet, when you hold onto that pain, you may unintentionally burden them with your unresolved emotions. Your partner, your friends, your family, they may find themselves dealing with the fallout of your past, even though they had no part in it.

This is why healing is so essential, not just for yourself but for the people around you. When you heal, you're not only freeing yourself from the grip of old wounds, but you're also allowing yourself to be the best version of you for the people who matter most. You're showing up as someone who can love, support, and connect with others in a healthy, meaningful way, without the shadows of the past clouding the present.

Ask yourself: What have I been suppressing? What pain am I carrying that I haven't fully dealt with? These questions aren't easy to answer, but they're necessary for healing. Maybe it's old heartbreak that still lingers, or past trauma that you've never fully confronted. Whatever it is, avoiding it won't make it disappear. It will continue to affect your relationships, your interactions, and even your own sense of peace until you take the time to address it.

Healing doesn't mean forgetting what happened or pretending the pain wasn't real. It means acknowledging it, processing it, and letting it go so that it no longer controls you. It's about taking responsibility for your own emotional well-being and recognizing that the people around you deserve the best version of you, the one that isn't weighed down by unresolved hurt.

It's also about forgiveness, not just forgiving others, but forgiving yourself for holding onto pain for so long. Healing is an act of self-love, and by choosing to heal, you're choosing to create healthier, stronger relationships with the people who care about you.

The people who love you want to see you thrive, not struggle under the weight of old wounds. They deserve to experience you at your best, free from the past, open to the present, and ready to build a future without the shadows of unresolved pain. And more importantly, you deserve that, too. You deserve to live without the heaviness of old hurt dictating how you move through life.

So, take the time to heal. Address the pain you've been suppressing. Not for anyone else, but for yourself. And in doing so, you'll also be giving a gift to those who love you, a version of you that's whole, present, and fully capable of loving and being loved without the past getting in the way.

Acknowledge suffering

Most of our pain comes from our own doing. It's a difficult truth to confront, but when we pause and reflect, we often find that the root of many of our problems is in the choices we make, the actions we take, or the thoughts we allow to fester. It's easy to place blame on circumstances, other people, or even bad luck, but when we dig deeper, we begin to see a different picture. Often, we are the architects of our own struggles, whether consciously or unconsciously. The sooner we come to terms with this, the sooner we can start to grow and move forward.

Have you ever stopped to consider how many of the challenges you face stem from decisions you've made or actions you've taken? The arguments that linger because of words spoken in anger, the missed opportunities because of procrastination or fear, the stress that builds from overcommitting yourself to things that don't truly align with your values, these are just a few examples of how we contribute to our own pain. But rather than facing this, we often deflect or deny it, choosing to blame external factors.

Yet, there's power in realizing that if we are responsible for much of our pain, we also hold the power to change it. The moment you take responsibility for your actions, the moment you stop seeing yourself as a victim of circumstances, you begin to reclaim control over your life. Admitting that you've made mistakes isn't a sign of weakness; it's a sign of maturity, of growth. It shows that you're willing to look at the hard truths and take the necessary steps to correct them.

Taking responsibility is not about self-blame, nor is it about drowning in guilt. It's about understanding the role you've played in creating your current situation and, more importantly, what you can do differently moving forward. Accountability is the key to breaking the cycle of repeating the same mistakes. When you accept that your actions, whether through poor decisions, impulsive reactions, or misguided thoughts, have contributed to where you are now, you give yourself the opportunity to choose a different path.

Think about this: If you continue to avoid responsibility, you're giving your power away. You're allowing the same patterns to persist, the same mistakes to be made, and the same pain to follow you. But when you own up to your part in the problem, you take back the steering wheel of your life. You begin to see where you went wrong and, more importantly, how to make things right.

Progress comes when you stop running from the truth and start facing it head-on. It's not about perfection or never making mistakes again, it's about learning, evolving, and becoming better with each misstep. When you take accountability for the pain you've caused yourself, you're also taking the first step toward healing and growth. It's a journey of self-awareness that frees you from being stuck in the past and empowers you to move forward with greater wisdom.

Ask yourself: Where have I contributed to my own pain? What actions or decisions have led me here? And how can I take responsibility for my role in this? The answers to these questions may be uncomfortable, but they are the first steps toward real progress. When you stop seeing your pain as something that happens to you and start recognizing it as something you have the power to change, everything shifts.

In the end, acknowledging your role in your own suffering isn't about dwelling on mistakes, it's about giving yourself the chance to learn from them. It's about realizing that while you may have created some of your problems, you also have the power to solve them. By taking responsibility, you allow yourself to make better choices, to act with intention, and to move forward with the strength that comes from knowing you are in control of your own life.

Chapter 33

Accountability

When we recognize what we can control, it becomes easier to make choices that honour our values, respect our boundaries, and allow us to grow. It's through this approach that we learn to balance empathy with self-respect, let go of situations that no longer align with who we are, and ultimately create a life that reflects what we truly want.

This statement reflects a powerful call to set clear boundaries and honour our own time. Often, we invest energy into people or situations that don't value our efforts. If someone has shown disregard for our time, learning from this experience is a form of growth. Accountability requires looking inward, examining why we may have allowed our time to be compromised. Were we seeking approval, overlooking red flags, or hoping for change?

By understanding these motivations, we can break the cycle of repeated disappointment. This isn't about cutting people off at the first sign of trouble; it's about valuing our own time enough to avoid patterns that lead to feeling unappreciated. Empathy is crucial here, as it allows us to forgive others without compromising our boundaries. Setting boundaries allows us to learn from experiences while still showing understanding and growth, ultimately protecting our time and emotional well-being.

When someone shows they're comfortable with your absence, it's tempting to fight for their attention or commitment. However, relationships should be reciprocal. When we're giving more than we're receiving, accountability helps us understand that continually fighting for someone who doesn't value us is ultimately a disservice to our own well-being. Respecting others' choices, even when it means stepping back, is a form of honouring both their autonomy and our own boundaries.

Empathy, in this context, means understanding without enabling. Letting someone go doesn't mean we lack compassion; it means we respect their choices as well as our own needs. If someone is willing to let us go, respecting that decision without compromising our self-worth allows us to create space for people who genuinely value and cherish our presence. Knowing when to stop fighting is a powerful step in embracing relationships based on mutual respect.

By taking responsibility for our actions, behaviours, and decisions, we begin to understand our motivations on a deeper level. Accountability enables us to recognize patterns and triggers that influence our choices. For example, instead of blaming others for conflicts, we can look inward, acknowledge our role, and make adjustments to foster healthier dynamics.

People who take ownership of their actions are better equipped to communicate openly and relate to others with empathy. They approach situations with a sense of emotional intelligence, building trust and creating environments where both people feel valued and respected. Accountability strengthens relationships by fostering transparency and a genuine commitment to growth. It's an essential part of meaningful connections, where each person's contributions are seen and appreciated.

One of the most freeing realizations is that we don't need to control everything around us; rather, we have the power to choose our actions and responses. When we fixate on trying to control external circumstances, we end up frustrated and disappointed. Instead, by focusing on our own choices and responses, we find peace and stability, creating outcomes that are within our reach.

Accountability here means taking ownership of our responses, ensuring that we're acting in alignment with our values and not trying to force others to change. When we let go of the need to control everything around us, we free ourselves from frustration. This clarity helps us focus on what we can influence, allowing us to build resilience, act thoughtfully, and make choices that bring fulfilment. In this way, we find true freedom, grounded in the understanding that our actions, rather than external events shape the quality of our lives.

Each of these concepts ultimately reflects the importance of accountability and respect in leading a fulfilling, balanced life. When we take responsibility for our actions and choices, we can set healthy boundaries, foster reciprocal relationships, and approach situations with empathy and wisdom. Accountability is the foundation of personal growth, guiding us to make choices that reflect our true values and inner strength.

As we become more accountable, we're better equipped to handle life's challenges, knowing that every experience offers an opportunity to learn. We see our mistakes not as failures but as steps toward becoming our best selves. We recognize our patterns, hold ourselves accountable, and extend the same grace to others that we offer ourselves.

In relationships, accountability allows us to love with openness and compassion while still protecting our boundaries. It teaches us to value our time and energy, to let go of those who don't appreciate us, and to focus on what we can control. When we live with accountability, we align our actions with our values, creating a life that reflects who we truly are.

Ultimately, accountability is a path to inner peace and authentic connection. It frees us from the need to seek external validation, empowering us to live in a way that honours our deepest truths. Through accountability and respect, we learn that every experience, whether challenging or joyful, contributes to our growth, shaping us into the people we're meant to become.

Foster curiosity

Curiosity is like a flame, and for it to burn brightly, it needs to be nurtured. As parents, teachers, or mentors, one of the most powerful things you can do is to reward and encourage a child's love for new things. When children's curiosity is met with excitement, support, and acknowledgment, it grows into a lifelong love of learning. They begin to see that exploration and discovery aren't just allowed, they're celebrated. And this creates a spark that will carry them through every stage of their development.

Curiosity doesn't just appear out of nowhere. It's fostered when children feel safe and encouraged to ask questions, make mistakes, and explore the world in new ways. Imagine the difference between a child who is met with a simple "don't touch" or "because I said so" and a child who is invited to ask "why?" or "how does this work?" The first child may back away, learning to accept things as they are. The second child feels empowered to dig deeper, to question, and to uncover new layers of understanding. They feel that their natural love for new things is something valuable.

The simple act of rewarding a child's curiosity can take many forms. It's not just about giving praise, but about truly engaging with them in their discoveries. When they show an interest in something, show them that their curiosity matters. Whether it's through encouraging their questions, exploring ideas together, or providing resources to fuel their interests, you're telling them that their desire to learn is important. This affirmation helps children develop the confidence to follow their own path of discovery, knowing they are supported.

By rewarding curiosity, you create a learning environment where children are excited to explore new things, instead of fearing they might get something wrong. They stop seeing learning as a chore and begin to associate it with adventure, with wonder, and with joy. And when children are allowed to engage with the world in this way, their minds stay open to endless possibilities.

Consider how this approach transforms a child's relationship with learning. Instead of memorizing facts for the sake of getting the right answer, they start to engage with the "why" and the "how" behind everything they learn. They develop a hunger for new knowledge, not because it's expected of them, but because they've come to find joy in the process.

Imagine the lasting impact of this mindset: a child whose curiosity is nurtured and rewarded grows into an adult who loves learning, who is resilient in the face of challenges, and who sees the world as a place full of endless possibilities. They become innovators, problem solvers, and creative thinkers, people who contribute not just by repeating what they know, but by discovering new ways to approach life's complexities.

So, foster curiosity in your children by celebrating their love for new things. Let them know that their questions, ideas, and explorations are important. When you reward their curiosity, you plant the seeds of a lifelong passion for discovery. This is how you create not just learners, but individuals who feel empowered to explore, question, and transform the world around them.

Live with integrity

Someone who lives with integrity will always attract others with integrity. This is a law of the universe, a powerful, unspoken truth that governs the way we connect with the world and the people around us. When you choose to live authentically, with honesty and integrity at the core of everything you do, you naturally attract others who value and live by those same principles. The energy you put out into the world is mirrored back to you, and those who resonate with that energy will find their way into your life.

Integrity is not just about being honest; it's about being true to yourself, standing by your values, and doing what's right even when no one is watching. It means living in alignment with who you are, not compromising your beliefs for the sake of convenience, approval, or success. This kind of authenticity radiates a powerful energy that others can feel, even if they don't fully understand it. People with integrity are drawn to others who are genuine, because they recognize something familiar and trustworthy in them.

The universe operates on the principle of energy alignment. The kind of energy you project, whether it is honesty, compassion, kindness, or integrity, will determine the kind of people and situations you attract into your life. When you live with integrity, you create a space for others who share your values to enter. You'll find that as you continue to walk your path with integrity, the people who don't align with that energy will naturally drift away, making room for those who do.

Living with integrity isn't always easy. There will be times when you feel challenged, when taking the high road seems difficult or isolating. You may even feel like you're walking your path alone for a while, as those who don't share your values begin to fade from your life. But this is where the law of the universe comes into play: those who are meant for you, those who live with the same level of integrity, will come into your life when you need them most. These are the people who will respect your truth, honour your journey, and offer you the same level of authenticity in return.

When you live with integrity, you become a magnet for others who do the same. You build relationships based on mutual respect, honesty, and trust, connections that are real, deep, and lasting. These relationships aren't built on superficial charm or fleeting interests; they're grounded in shared values and a genuine respect for each other's truth.

The beauty of living with integrity is that it not only attracts people of the same caliber, but it also encourages others to live more authentically themselves. Your actions, your words, and the way you carry yourself become a quiet inspiration for those around you. People see your integrity and feel drawn to rise to the same level of honesty and authenticity in their own lives. This is how integrity spreads, how it creates a ripple effect in the world.

So, trust that living with integrity is not just about personal fulfilment, it's a law of the universe that guarantees you will attract people who value and embody the same principles. The right people, opportunities, and experiences will naturally flow into your life as long as you stay true to who you are. You don't need to compromise or chase after relationships that don't align with your values. Live authentically, with integrity at the heart of everything you do, and the universe will ensure that you are surrounded by others who do the same.

Chapter 34

Strengthen your faith

"No eye has seen, no ear has heard, no mind has conceived what God has prepared for those who love him." This profound message reminds us that there is a greater plan at work, something beyond what we can even imagine, waiting for us when we live in alignment with faith and trust. But this is not just about divine grace; it's also about the immense potential that lies within you. The universe is a reflection of who you are, and when you believe in your own worth and strength, extraordinary things are possible.

Take a moment to consider this: What if everything you desire, everything you dream of, is already within your reach, just waiting for you to claim it? The universe operates on a principle of reflection. What you put out into the world, your thoughts, your beliefs, your energy, comes back to you. When you strengthen your faith in yourself, in your potential, and in the unseen forces working in your favour, you unlock doors you didn't even know existed.

Often, we limit ourselves by what we can see or understand. We get caught in the daily struggles, convinced that our lives are confined to the small moments of disappointment or fear. But this quote serves as a reminder that there is something so much greater at play. You are part of a vast, intricate design, and when you align yourself with faith, both in the universe and in your own abilities, anything becomes possible.

Ask yourself: Do you truly believe in your own potential? Do you trust that the universe is working with you, not against you? Many of us walk through life doubting ourselves, thinking that the possibilities for our future are limited by what we see in the present. But this belief keeps you small. It keeps you from fully realizing the power you hold within. The truth is, the universe reflects back to you the faith you have in yourself. When you start to believe that you are capable of greatness, the universe responds by opening paths, bringing opportunities, and aligning events to help you succeed.

Strengthening your faith in yourself doesn't mean you have to know exactly how everything will unfold. It means trusting that even if you don't see the full picture yet, there is something far greater ahead. It means understanding that your thoughts, your actions, and your mindset create the world you experience. The universe is always mirroring your inner state.

If you think small, the universe reflects that. If you doubt yourself, it mirrors that too. But when you start to believe in the boundless possibilities that are already waiting for you, when you trust that you are deserving of all the beauty and success the universe has to offer, you begin to see those reflections in your life.

Faith is not just about belief in something external, like a higher power; it's also about belief in yourself, that you are worthy of everything you desire, that your dreams have a place in this world, and that your life is unfolding in perfect timing. The universe is constantly responding to who you are and what you believe about yourself.

So, strengthen your faith, not just in what's unseen but in the very core of who you are. Know that the universe is reflecting back your greatness, your potential, and your worth. There is more waiting for you than you can even imagine, and it's all within reach when you believe in yourself and trust the journey. The possibilities are endless, and the universe is just waiting for you to embrace them.

Embrace small things

It's the small things that often go unnoticed, but they are the threads that weave "contentment" into our lives. Sometimes we get so caught up in trying to meet external expectations, what others think we should like, what seems popular, or what we think will make us more accepted, that we lose sight of what truly makes us happy. But deep contentment doesn't come from living up to someone else's standards. It comes from the little things that resonate with you, the things that make your heart lighter and your mind more at peace.

Have you ever stopped to ask yourself: What do I genuinely enjoy? What brings me that quiet sense of joy, without the need for validation from others? Often, we overlook these small, personal joys in favour of what's more socially acceptable or what seems "cool." But the truth is, those small things, the morning cup of coffee brewed just how you like it, the favourite song that plays on repeat, the smell of rain, the quiet moment spent alone in nature, those are the moments where real contentment begins.

It's easy to get caught up in what others enjoy and think that, because they find pleasure in something, you should too. But the key to true contentment is realizing that your preferences, your small joys, don't have to match anyone else's. You don't have to like the latest trends or adopt popular hobbies to feel validated. You only need to tune into yourself and embrace what feels right for you.

Think about the things that truly make you feel alive, not because others find them exciting, but because you do. Maybe it's the way you spend your Sunday mornings, with a book in hand and no obligations, or the thrill you get from learning something new, even if no one else shares that passion. Maybe it's a simple walk through your neighbourhood, the smell of freshly baked bread, or the quiet satisfaction of completing a personal project. These are the little things that hold real value, even if no one else notices them.

Ask yourself: Am I doing things because I truly enjoy them, or because I think I'm supposed to? Am I chasing external approval, or am I following the quiet pull of my own happiness? When you start answering these questions, you'll discover that the path to real contentment is much simpler than you might have thought. It's about choosing the things that matter to you.

Contentment isn't found in grand gestures or living according to others' expectations. It's in the small, everyday moments that bring you joy, the ones that feel right to you, even if they seem insignificant to others. Your preferences don't need to match anyone else's because the things that bring you contentment are yours alone.

So, embrace the small things. Find comfort in your own preferences, no matter how different they may seem from the crowd. In the end, contentment comes from living authentically, from choosing the things that make you feel whole. It's the small, seemingly ordinary moments that are often the most extraordinary when they come from a place of true personal joy. And that's where real happiness resides not in what others think you should enjoy, but in what makes your heart truly sing.

Earth's time is limited

Your time on Earth is limited, but you don't need to make drastic changes to live a life worth remembering. You don't have to move across the world, reinvent yourself completely, or abandon everything you know to create a story full of adventure and meaning. Life isn't about dramatic transformations; it's about the small, intentional shifts that bring richness and depth to your everyday existence. Even the simplest changes can open up new worlds of experience and growth.

We often think that in order to live a more exciting or fulfilling life, we need to make huge leaps quit our jobs, chase radical goals, or take risks that feel almost impossible. But in reality, adventure and fulfilment often come in the form of small, manageable changes. A different way of looking at the world, a new hobby, a slight shift in how you approach each day, all of these can add up to create a life that feels expansive and full of possibilities.

Ask yourself: what small changes could you make that would bring more excitement, curiosity, and meaning to your life? Maybe it's as simple as reading a book on a subject you've always been curious about, exploring a new part of your city, or striking up a conversation with someone you've never really spoken to. These small acts of exploration can gradually reshape your life, broadening your horizons without overwhelming you.

Embracing change doesn't have to be overwhelming. You can start right where you are, with the tools you already have. The goal isn't to become someone entirely different, but to gently push the boundaries of what feels comfortable and familiar. These small steps allow you to expand your world in a way that feels natural and achievable. And as you do, you'll begin to see how even minor adjustments can lead to new insights, experiences, and a richer understanding of yourself and the world around you.

You don't need to upend your life to feel alive. The beauty of growth and adventure is that they often happen in subtle, everyday moments.

It's in the decision to try something new, to view a situation from a different perspective, or to take a step outside your routine. Over time, these small, consistent changes create a sense of momentum, helping you live with more intention, curiosity, and excitement.

Let go of the idea that a more fulfilling life requires drastic change. Instead, embrace the power of small, deliberate actions that allow you to explore, grow, and evolve. Your story doesn't need to be filled with massive transformations, it just needs to be filled with moments of discovery, moments where you chose to see the world a little differently or to embrace something new.

Age with a story that's yours, one built not on dramatic leaps, but on the steady, meaningful steps you take each day. Let those small changes add richness to your life, and watch how they turn into the adventures you'll remember. Life doesn't have to be radical to be extraordinary; sometimes the most profound shifts come from simply being open to the possibilities each day brings.

Chapter 35

Willing to let go

There's something deeply powerful in this statement. Think of the way a bird soars effortlessly through the sky, free from the weight that keeps it grounded. Now, imagine yourself with wings, your potential, your dreams, your highest self, all ready to take flight. But instead of rising, you feel held back, tethered to the ground by unseen forces. Have you ever wondered what's weighing you down? What is it that keeps you from moving forward, from fully embracing the life you desire?

It's easy to get stuck in the routine of life, burdened by things we might not even realize are holding us back. It could be the fear of failure, relationships that no longer serve us, or habits that keep us from growing. The more you carry these weights, the heavier they become, and the more difficult it is to move toward your goals. But to truly progress, to "fly" in life, you need to let go of what no longer serves you.

Take a moment to reflect: what's holding you back? Is it self-doubt? Are you constantly questioning your abilities, worrying that you're not good enough? Self-doubt is like a heavy chain wrapped around your wings. Every time you try to rise, it pulls you back down, reminding you of all the reasons you "think" you can't succeed. But the truth is, self-doubt is an illusion. It's not a reflection of your capabilities, but of the fears you've accumulated over time. The more you believe in those fears, the harder it becomes to break free.

Perhaps it's the fear of what others think. How often do you find yourself adjusting your dreams, your decisions, or your actions based on the opinions of those around you? This fear can be crippling, keeping you stuck in place because you're too afraid of judgment or rejection. But living for others' approval will always keep you grounded. It's only when you give yourself permission to live authentically, without the need for external validation that you begin to soar.

Another common weight that holds people down is the baggage of past experiences. Maybe it's a mistake you made, a failure you endured, or a relationship that hurt you. Carrying these past experiences like a burden keeps you from progressing, because you're constantly looking backward, reliving the pain, instead of focusing on where you want to go. To fly, you must learn to let go of the past, to release yourself from the grip it has on your present.

Then, there are the toxic relationships or environments that drain your energy. You might have people in your life who don't support your growth, who keep you small because your progress makes them uncomfortable. These relationships act like anchors, preventing you from rising to your full potential. It's difficult to fly when you're surrounded by people who constantly pull you down. Letting go of these relationships, though difficult, is essential if you want to move forward.

Now, think about the habits or distractions that hold you back. Are there routines you're stuck in that keep you from progressing? It might be procrastination, avoiding the hard work, or filling your time with distractions to avoid confronting your goals. These habits weigh you down, trapping you in a cycle of stagnation. Letting go of them requires discipline, but it also creates space for real growth and change.

The key to flying in life is not to hold onto everything, but to release what no longer serves you. Imagine what would happen if you let go of self-doubt, the fear of judgment, the weight of your past, or the relationships that no longer support you. Imagine how much lighter you'd feel, how much more space you'd have to rise. The higher you want to go, the less you can carry with you. The more you release, the more you realize that you have always had the ability to soar.

It's time to identify what's weighing you down, to confront it, and to make the conscious choice to let it go. It's not always easy, but the freedom that comes with releasing these weights is worth the effort. When you let go of what holds you back, you give yourself permission to rise into your fullest potential, to embrace the life you've always dreamed of.

To fly, you must be free. And to be free, you must be willing to let go. The question is: what are you holding onto, and are you ready to release it? The sky is waiting for you, are you ready to rise?

Right people appreciate

You don't need to make sense of everyone. The right people will appreciate you for who you are, not for who they want you to be."

Take a moment and consider why so many of us feel the need to be understood, accepted, and validated by everyone we meet. It's a common human desire, we want to belong, to feel seen, and to be loved for who we are. But in this pursuit, we often forget that not everyone is meant to understand or even accept us. We bend, shift, and mould ourselves into different versions just to fit into expectations that were never ours to begin with. But is that really the life you want to live?

Let's take this journey deeper. Think about the people in your life who don't quite get you. Maybe it's because of your choices, your personality, or the way you see the world. Their misunderstanding may leave you feeling judged, or like you're falling short of some invisible standard. But ask yourself: are you really willing to change who you are to gain the approval of people who don't see you for who you truly are? Or, more importantly, is their approval even worth having?

The real question is, why do we chase this approval in the first place? Why do we feel the need to make sense of ourselves in the eyes of everyone, even those who don't resonate with us? Maybe it's fear, fear of rejection, of being misunderstood, or of standing out. Maybe we're taught that fitting in is safer than standing in our truth. But the truth is, this constant need to make sense to others comes at a price, the price of authenticity.

When you shape-shift for others, you lose yourself in the process. You start to dim your light to fit into spaces that were never meant for you. But here's the thing: the people who are meant to be in your life, the ones who matter, will never ask you to change who you are. They will see your full self, your strengths, your flaws, your quirks and they will love you for it. Not despite it.

Imagine what it would feel like to live without the burden of trying to make everyone understand you. To no longer feel the weight of expectation that forces you to prove yourself to people who were never going to see you fully anyway. The people who really matter, the right people, will appreciate you not just for who you are, but for who you are not. They won't need you to fill a mould or play a role. They'll accept the parts of you that don't align with their own worldview, because they see your essence, not just the surface.

Ask yourself: Do you really want to be surrounded by people who only love you conditionally, based on how well you fit into their image of what's acceptable? Or would you rather be loved and appreciated for the whole of who you are, including the parts that might not make sense to others? When you stop trying to make sense to everyone, you allow space for the people who truly see you to come closer. You create room for genuine connections built on understanding, not on forcing yourself into someone else's narrow expectations.

In letting go of the need to be understood by everyone, you open the door to a more authentic life. You stop chasing approval, and you start attracting the right people, people who appreciate your depth, your complexity, and even the parts of you that might seem contradictory or hard to pin down. These are the people who will see you for who you are, and for who you aren't. They won't need to fit you into a box or label you according to their limited perceptions.

The conclusion is clear: not everyone will understand you, and that's perfectly fine. The right people will. They'll appreciate the full spectrum of who you are, not just the parts that are easy to accept. And once you embrace this, you'll realize that the people worth having in your life are the ones who don't need you to make sense to them. They'll simply love and accept you as you are.

Stronger than pain

Are you healed, or just trying not to think about it? This question cuts deep, doesn't it? It forces you to pause and reflect on how you've been handling your pain. So often, we convince ourselves that by pushing things to the back of our minds, we're "over it." We tuck away the hurt, the memories, and the unresolved emotions, thinking that if we don't focus on them, they'll eventually disappear. But the truth is, ignoring something doesn't mean it's healed. It's still there, beneath the surface, waiting for a quiet moment to remind you that it hasn't really gone away.

Healing is not about avoidance. It's about confrontation, acceptance, and understanding. When you suppress your pain or try to distract yourself from it, you might feel temporary relief. But in reality, those emotions are still festering inside, affecting your mind, your heart, and even your body. They weigh you down in ways you might not even realize. So, ask yourself: Are you truly healed, or are you simply avoiding the things you don't want to deal with?

Confronting your pain is not easy. It requires courage and vulnerability. It means looking at the things you've tried to avoid, your mistakes, your wounds, your regrets and accepting that they are part of your story. But here's the thing: by acknowledging them, you take the first step toward real healing. Pushing them down only traps you in a cycle of numbness, never allowing you to fully move forward. You might feel "okay" on the surface, but underneath, the pain still lingers, affecting how you see the world and how you interact with it.

True healing happens when you stop running from your emotions and start processing them. This doesn't mean you have to confront everything at once; healing is a gradual journey. But it does mean giving yourself the space to feel, to grieve, and to let go. To heal is to allow yourself to be human, to acknowledge that you've been hurt and that it's okay to feel that pain. Once you do, you'll find that it doesn't control you the way it used to. It loses its power because you've faced it head-on, and in that confrontation, you take back your strength.

Consider what might change in your life if you stopped avoiding what's on your mind and actually dealt with it. Think about how much lighter you might feel. The energy you spend trying to push your emotions down could be redirected toward growth, toward creating the life you truly want. Imagine how freeing it would be to no longer carry those unhealed parts of yourself everywhere you go.

Healing doesn't mean the pain never happened. It means it no longer controls you. It's about integrating those difficult experiences into who you are, not as burdens, but as lessons that have shaped you. When you confront what's been holding you back, you free yourself from its grip. You stop being a prisoner to your past, and you start living more fully in the present.

You deserve to live without that heavy weight on your shoulders. But that freedom only comes when you stop pretending that avoiding the pain is the same as healing it. It's not. Avoidance keeps you stuck. Healing moves you forward. It's a hard journey, yes, but it's a transformative one. The moment you decide to stop pushing things away and start addressing them, you open the door to real change.

So, are you healed, or are you just trying not to think about it? Be honest with yourself. Life will get better when you choose healing over avoidance. You'll find peace, strength, and clarity that you didn't think were possible. And once you start that journey, you'll realize that the things you were so afraid to face weren't as powerful as you thought. You are stronger than your pain, and healing is within your reach, if you're willing to confront it.

Chapter 36

Believe in yourself

This is a natural law of the universe: when you start believing in yourself, the energy you put out shifts, and in turn, the world around you responds. It's as though the very fabric of existence is wired to react to the way we view ourselves. The universe is a mirror, reflecting back the confidence, belief, and self-worth you cultivate within. And when you believe in yourself, that energy ripples outward, attracting opportunities, people, and experiences that align with this new mindset.

At the core of this universal law is the understanding that your thoughts and beliefs shape your reality. When you carry doubt and fear, you unconsciously limit what you allow into your life. You attract circumstances that reflect that doubt, reinforcing the cycle. But when you flip the script and begin to see yourself as capable, worthy, and deserving of success and happiness, the universe takes notice. Opportunities that once seemed distant suddenly draw closer. People who align with your new energy naturally gravitate toward you. And challenges that once felt insurmountable become stepping stones for growth.

It's not magic, it's a law of energy and focus. What you believe about yourself sets the tone for the experiences you invite into your life. And this law extends beyond just personal success; it influences the people around you. When you live with self-belief, you inspire others to do the same. Your energy becomes contagious. Others start seeing what's possible for them by watching how you've transformed your own life. It's like throwing a stone into a still pond, your belief in yourself sends ripples far beyond what you can see.

We see this law play out everywhere in life. Those who believe in themselves naturally achieve more, not because they're luckier or more talented, but because they've unlocked the potential within themselves to attract and create opportunities. It's the same reason why those who radiate positivity and self-confidence often find that people are drawn to them. The universe rewards those who align their thoughts with their desires, and the first step in doing so is to believe that you're capable and deserving of what you want.

When you begin to embrace this truth, you'll notice how your external reality begins to reflect the inner work you're doing. Obstacles will still exist, but you'll approach them with a new sense of resilience and trust. Relationships will begin to shift, drawing people who truly support and uplift you. The more you believe in yourself, the more the universe responds by aligning the right circumstances in your favour.

So, understand that this is not a coincidence. It's not luck. It's the natural law of the universe at work. When you believe in yourself, you tap into a force that is far greater than you, one that brings everything in your life into harmony with your inner belief. Start trusting in this law, and you'll be amazed at what you can attract and achieve.

Excuses make tomorrow harder

Excuses make today easy but tomorrow harder. It's a comforting thought, to put things off, to tell ourselves we'll get to it later, or that now just isn't the right time. Excuses give us a temporary escape, a way to bypass discomfort or difficulty in the present. But with every excuse we make, we unknowingly burden our future. What seems like a harmless delay today can snowball into more stress, more pressure, and fewer opportunities tomorrow. We feel relief in the moment, but that relief is short-lived, because the things we avoid don't simply disappear. They accumulate, waiting for us with added weight.

When we rely on excuses, we make a trade-off: immediate comfort for future strain. Tasks get pushed aside, responsibilities are delayed, and our goals remain distant. It may seem like the easier path at first, after all, avoiding something uncomfortable feels like a win. But the reality is that what we choose not to face today often becomes more difficult to tackle later. The unfinished work piles up, the missed chances slip further away, and what could have been a simple challenge to address now becomes a looming obstacle down the line.

Think about those moments where you've delayed something important whether it's a project, a difficult conversation, or even a personal goal like getting healthier. In the moment, it feels easier to say, "I'll do it tomorrow." But tomorrow turns into next week, next month, and eventually, the delay makes the task seem insurmountable. Procrastination, fuelled by excuses, creates a cycle of avoidance that leaves us unprepared when the deadline finally arrives. By making excuses today, we only create more anxiety and pressure for our future selves.

On the flip side, discipline makes today hard but tomorrow easier. Discipline requires effort, focus, and often discomfort in the moment, but it's a long-term investment in your future. When you choose discipline over excuses, you're choosing to take on the challenges of today head-on, rather than postponing them for later. It may not feel easy in the moment, but every act of discipline strengthens your ability to grow and achieve more over time.

Discipline isn't about perfection, it's about consistency. It's showing up and doing the work even when it's hard, even when you'd rather take the easy way out. Every time you practice discipline, you're building momentum. It may feel like a struggle at first, but with time, it becomes easier. The things that once felt overwhelming start to feel more manageable. By putting in the work today, you create a smoother path for yourself tomorrow.

When you practice discipline, you are not only tackling today's tasks, but you are also setting yourself up for success in the future. For example, sticking to a fitness routine may feel exhausting today, but over time, your health improves, your energy increases, and what once felt difficult starts to feel natural. By being disciplined, you're investing in the future version of yourself, one who is stronger, more resilient, and better equipped to handle challenges.

Discipline also brings a sense of accomplishment and control over your life. Every time you push through discomfort and take action, you reinforce the belief that you are capable of doing hard things. This builds confidence, making future challenges feel less daunting. The more disciplined you are today, the easier it becomes to stay disciplined tomorrow, and that cycle creates progress that compounds over time.

Excuses, on the other hand, do the opposite. Each excuse you make chips away at your confidence. You start to doubt yourself, to question your ability to get things done. The longer you avoid something, the harder it feels to start. The task itself might not have changed, but your mindset around it has. What could have been handled with discipline becomes overwhelming because of the weight of missed opportunities and mounting pressure.

The contrast between excuses and discipline is stark. Excuses offer immediate comfort but at the cost of future stress and lost opportunities. Discipline demands effort now, but it sets you up for long-term success and fulfilment. The choice between the two shapes not just your day, but the quality of your life moving forward.

It's important to acknowledge that discipline doesn't mean you have to be perfect. There will be days when it's hard to push through, when excuses seem tempting. But the key is to return to discipline as often as possible. It's about making the choice, again and again, to prioritize long-term benefits over short-term relief. Every small act of discipline counts, and every excuse you resist makes the path ahead a little easier.

So, ask yourself: what kind of tomorrow do you want? A future where you feel burdened by the things you didn't handle today, or a future where you feel empowered by the progress you made? The decisions you make today determine how easy or difficult your tomorrow will be.

Choose discipline, not because it's easy, but because it's worth it. Each time you opt for discipline over excuses, you're taking control of your future, making it easier, lighter, and more fulfilling. The hard work you put in now will pay off, transforming your tomorrows into something better than you could have imagined.

Empowering thoughts

Ultimately, you are what you think. Every thought you allow into your mind shapes the way you see yourself, how you experience life, and how you respond to challenges. Your thoughts are powerful, they have the ability to build you up or tear you down, depending on what you choose to focus on. If you constantly feed yourself thoughts of self-doubt, shame, or guilt, those thoughts begin to take root and influence how you live, how you perceive yourself, and how you interact with the world. But if you consciously choose to fill your mind with kindness, patience, and self-compassion, your entire experience can shift.

Consider this: every belief you hold about yourself started as a thought. Maybe you once thought, "I'm not good enough" or "I don't deserve success," and over time, you began to believe these thoughts as if they were fact. The reality is, these beliefs are not inherent truths. They are just thoughts that you've repeated so often, they've become part of how you define yourself. The good news is that the reverse is also true, when you consistently think thoughts that support your growth, confidence, and self-worth, you begin to transform your sense of self and, ultimately, your life.

But how often do we let negative or limiting thoughts dominate our minds? We all have moments of insecurity, times when we question ourselves or feel like we're not measuring up. It's in those moments that your thoughts matter the most. When you catch yourself thinking, "I'm not capable" or "I'm failing," ask yourself: is this thought helping me? Is it serving my growth, or is it holding me back? Often, we don't realize how much power we give to our thoughts, letting them dictate how we feel about ourselves without questioning their validity.

You have the power to change your internal narrative. It starts with becoming aware of what you're thinking and recognizing the impact your thoughts have on your well-being. Instead of allowing negative thoughts to take over, make a conscious effort to challenge them. If you think, "I'm not good enough," try shifting that to, "I'm doing the best I can, and that's enough." If you find yourself saying, "I always mess things up," replace it with, "I'm learning, and it's okay to make mistakes."

When you begin to feed your mind with supportive, positive thoughts, your outlook changes. You start to see yourself as someone worthy of love, success, and happiness. Your confidence grows, not because everything is suddenly perfect, but because you believe in your ability to handle whatever comes your way. You become more resilient, more adaptable, and more compassionate toward yourself, and that changes everything.

This doesn't mean that difficult moments won't arise, or that you'll never have negative thoughts again. But the difference is how you respond to those moments. You'll begin to recognize that negative thoughts don't define you, they're just fleeting ideas that you can choose to let go of. You don't have to accept every thought that crosses your mind as truth. Instead, you can consciously decide which thoughts you will allow to shape your reality.

Ask yourself: What thoughts are currently shaping my life? Are they helping me grow, or are they keeping me stuck? Are they nurturing me, or are they tearing me down? These questions help you become more mindful of your thinking patterns, allowing you to take control of how you experience life.

When you understand that your thoughts create your reality, you begin to realize how important it is to be kind to yourself. It's easy to fall into the trap of self-criticism, thinking it will push you to do better or be better. But true growth comes from a place of self-compassion, not harsh judgment. Being kind to yourself allows you to create a space where you can grow, learn, and improve without tearing yourself down in the process.

Remember, you are what you think. So choose thoughts that empower you, that remind you of your worth and potential. The more you focus on positive, supportive thinking, the more your reality will reflect the person you're becoming, a person who is capable, deserving, and resilient. You hold the power to shape your life with your thoughts. Use that power wisely, and you'll see just how much you can transform your world.

Chapter 37

Embrace hardships

In life, we often face moments of hardship and loss, whether it's a personal setback, a failed relationship, a missed opportunity, or an unexpected challenge. These experiences can be painful and difficult to process, but they hold within them valuable lessons that we should not overlook. Every loss, every struggle, carries an opportunity for growth. The key is to shift your focus from the loss itself to what you can learn from it.

During times of hardship, it's natural to feel overwhelmed, frustrated, or defeated. It's easy to focus on the pain or the immediate impact of the situation and overlook the deeper insights it offers. However, these difficult moments often teach us more about ourselves, our resilience, and our path in life than the easy or successful times ever could. In every loss, there is a hidden lesson, a chance to reflect, grow, and ultimately become stronger.

The lesson may come in the form of learning about your own strengths and weaknesses, gaining a new perspective, or understanding what really matters in your life. Perhaps it's a reminder of the importance of patience, or a lesson in perseverance, or maybe it teaches you how to let go of something that wasn't serving you. Regardless of the specifics, there is always something valuable to be gained if you look beyond the immediate disappointment.

It's important to realize that losing doesn't make you a failure; it's a necessary part of growth. The most successful people in life didn't get there without enduring setbacks, failures, and losses. What sets them apart is their ability to learn from those experiences. They don't let failure define them, they let it refine them. Each time they fall, they get back up, equipped with the lessons learned from their previous mistakes, and continue to move forward.

Life is a constant process of learning, and every experience, whether positive or negative, offers an opportunity to grow. When we lose, it's not the loss itself that defines us, but how we respond to it. If we choose to see the lesson within the loss, we turn every hardship into a stepping stone toward personal growth. When we allow ourselves to reflect on what went wrong, what we could have done differently, and what we can take away from the situation, we emerge stronger and more prepared for the future.

The truth is, there can be a lesson in everything. Every challenge, every failure, every loss contains a seed of wisdom waiting to be uncovered. Even in moments that feel devastating, there is always something to learn about yourself, about life, and about the world around you. The lesson may not always be immediately clear, but with time, reflection, and an open heart, it will reveal itself.

So, when you lose, don't lose the lesson. Embrace hardship as an opportunity for growth, knowing that within every setback lies a valuable lesson. Learn from it, grow from it, and carry those lessons forward with you. By doing so, you turn loss into wisdom, and setbacks into stepping stones toward a more resilient and empowered version of yourself.

Lifted from dark moments

A healer is someone who seeks the light they wished they had in their darkest moments. They are people who have walked through pain so deep, so consuming, that they know exactly what it feels like to be lost in the shadows. Healers aren't born into their role by accident; their journey to heal others often starts with the pain they've had to overcome themselves. They've felt the sting of loneliness, the weight of sadness, the ache of heartbreak, and instead of letting that pain break them, they used it to transform themselves. In doing so, they now seek to be the light for others who are struggling in the same darkness.

Healers are sensitive to the suffering around them because they've been there. They recognize the signs of hidden pain, of people trying to stay strong when they're barely holding on, because they've lived it. That's why they feel the pain of others so deeply, it resonates with something inside of them. It's not just empathy; it's a shared experience, a reminder of a past struggle that they understand in their bones. And because of that, they carry an unwavering desire to help others, to ensure no one has to feel the kind of loneliness or despair they once knew so well.

Imagine what kind of world we would live in without people who heal, who care so deeply about others that they make it their mission to uplift and support those in pain. Healers are the people who remind us that we don't have to face our battles alone, that there is someone who sees our hurt and is willing to help us carry it. They are the ones who listen when no one else does, who offer comfort without judgment, and who give us hope when we've lost sight of it. The world needs healers because they are the bridges between despair and hope, between hurt and healing.

Healers don't just tend to physical wounds; they address the emotional and spiritual scars that so often go unseen. They know that sometimes, the heaviest burdens we carry are the ones we hide from the world. They step in, offering love, support, and light in ways that go far beyond a simple act of kindness. To be a healer means to carry the weight of others' pain, not because it's easy, but because the healer knows what it's like to bear that pain alone.

But being a healer comes with its own challenges. Because they feel so deeply, they often carry the emotional weight of others' struggles. It's not easy to be so attuned to the suffering of the world, but healers do it because they understand that their ability to heal is a gift that the world desperately needs. They give of themselves so others can find their way back to the light.

Healers are the unsung heroes of our world. They don't wear capes or seek recognition, but their impact is profound. They remind us of our capacity for kindness, compassion, and resilience. They show us that even in the darkest times, there is light to be found. And for those who are lost, healers are the ones who help guide them back to a place of peace and understanding. The world needs healers now more than ever people who turn their own pain into a force of healing for others, who see the suffering and say, "I will help you through this, because I know how it feels, and I don't want you to go through it alone."

If you ever wonder if healers are needed, just look around. Every person who has been lifted out of their darkness, every heart that has been mended, and every soul that has been restored has been touched by someone who made it their mission to heal. That is the power and the beauty of a healer.

Never chase and expect

Never chase, never expect, never overshare, and never beg. It's a simple principle, but deeply transformative once you embrace it. So many of us spend our time chasing things we believe we need, whether it's love, approval, success, or recognition. We fall into the trap of thinking that by chasing, expecting, or oversharing, we will somehow force the universe to deliver what we want. But the truth is, what's meant for you will come to you when the time is right, and there's no need to push or beg for it.

One of the biggest misconceptions we carry is the belief that we need something outside of ourselves to be whole, to be fulfilled, or to be happy. We chase after these external validations, hoping that once we have them, we'll finally feel complete. But this mindset can leave us feeling anxious, frustrated, and empty, because the more we chase, the more distant these things seem. The act of chasing sends the message that we are lacking something and that we are not enough as we are.

Instead, the real work lies within. The more you focus on your inner growth on becoming the best, most authentic version of yourself the more you begin to attract what is truly meant for you. The energy you carry and the beliefs you hold create the space for opportunities, relationships, and experiences to flow into your life naturally. When you stop chasing and start trusting that what is meant for you will come, you shift from a place of lack to a place of abundance.

Never expect, because expectation breeds disappointment. When you attach your happiness to a specific outcome, you are handing over your power to something outside of your control. Life doesn't unfold according to a script, and expecting certain things to happen the way you envision them will only create frustration. Instead, embrace a mindset of trust and openness. Let go of rigid expectations and allow life to surprise you. Often, what's waiting for you is better than anything you could have planned.

Never overshare, because your journey is yours alone. There is strength in keeping parts of your life private. Oversharing can dilute the power of your experiences and open you up to unnecessary judgment or misunderstanding. It's important to protect your energy, to nurture your own growth, and to share only when it feels right, with people who truly value you.

And finally, never beg, because begging implies that you don't believe you're worthy. Whether it's begging for love, validation, or success, when you lower yourself to that level, you are diminishing your own value. You are enough as you are, and the things meant for you will recognize that worth. You don't have to beg for what's already aligned with your path.

The universe works in ways that we often don't understand. By doing the inner work by focusing on your growth, your peace, and your authenticity, you naturally attract what is meant for you. There's no need to chase, expect, or beg. Trust the process, trust yourself, and know that everything that's meant for you is on its way. Focus on becoming the person who's ready to receive it.

Chapter 38

Master your inner world

In every moment, regardless of external circumstances, you hold the power to shape your inner world through your thoughts, beliefs, and choices. This understanding is transformative, because it means that no matter what happens around you, your internal experience is something you can actively create. By choosing thoughts that uplift, beliefs that empower, and a mindset that aligns with love, you can cultivate a beautiful inner world that supports and nourishes your spirit.

Your thoughts are like seeds, and what you plant in your mind grows into the landscape of your life. If you plant seeds of doubt, fear, or negativity, they will manifest as feelings of unease, stress, or dissatisfaction. But when you plant thoughts of love, gratitude, and positivity, your inner world begins to bloom with peace, joy, and strength. You have the ability to choose what takes root in your mind, and that choice is incredibly powerful.

Beliefs, too, shape your inner experience. The beliefs you hold about yourself and the world around you create the framework through which you interpret everything. If you believe that life is full of opportunities and that you are deserving of love and happiness, your reality will reflect that belief. On the other hand, if you believe that life is full of struggle or that you are unworthy, you may find yourself stuck in those patterns. Choosing beliefs that support your growth and your divine energy is essential for creating an inner world that feels like home.

It's not always easy to choose love and positivity, especially in difficult times, but it is always possible. The key is to be intentional about how you respond to the challenges of life. You can choose to see setbacks as opportunities for growth, failures as lessons, and uncertainty as a doorway to possibility. You can choose to let go of thoughts that drain your energy and instead focus on thoughts that empower you. The choice is always yours, and with practice, it becomes second nature.

Choosing a path that feels like love means aligning your thoughts, feelings, and actions with what nourishes and supports your soul. It means being kind to yourself, practicing self-compassion, and surrounding yourself with energy that uplifts and protects your divine essence. When you choose love, you are not only supporting your own well-being but also protecting your sacred energy from negativity and stress. This path allows you to radiate peace, attract positivity, and maintain a deep connection with your inner truth.

Ultimately, you are the master of your inner world. You get to decide what thoughts and beliefs guide your journey. By choosing to cultivate thoughts that feel like love, you create a sanctuary within yourself, a place where your spirit can thrive no matter what happens in the external world. So choose wisely. Choose love, gratitude, and positivity. Choose to protect your divine energy, and you will create a life filled with joy, peace, and purpose.

Anger is self-punishment

Anger is the punishment we give ourselves for someone else's mistake. Often, at the heart of our anger is the desire to control something that is simply beyond our reach, someone else's actions, choices, or the outcome of a situation. Anger arises when we feel that things should have gone differently or that people should have behaved better. But the truth is, many things in life simply cannot be controlled, and trying to do so only leads to frustration and pain.

When we get angry, we're usually reacting to something outside of our control. Maybe someone hurt us, maybe a situation didn't go as planned, or perhaps someone's actions felt unfair. The natural response is to feel upset, even enraged, because we want things to change. But here's the hard truth: no amount of anger can undo what's already happened. No amount of frustration can change how someone else acts or force the situation to resolve the way you want it to. Anger, in this way, is futile, it is energy spent on trying to control the uncontrollable.

Understanding that some things cannot be controlled is the first step toward releasing anger. Life is unpredictable. People make mistakes. Circumstances change. Trying to control every outcome or every person's behaviour is an impossible task, and it's one that only leads to more suffering. Anger arises when we resist this reality, when we try to force our will onto something or someone that is out of our influence.

When you realize that there are things you simply cannot control, you begin to see how pointless holding onto anger can be. The mistake has already been made. The situation has already happened. Rather than punishing yourself with anger, you can choose acceptance. Acceptance doesn't mean agreeing with what happened or condoning someone's actions, it means recognizing that the only thing you can control is your response.

Letting go of the need for control is freeing. Instead of focusing on what went wrong or how you wish things were different, you focus on what you can change: your thoughts, your emotions, and your own actions. By doing this, you release yourself from the chains of anger, which often keep you stuck in a cycle of frustration and resentment.

Some things in life will never be within our control, and that's okay. Accepting this truth allows you to move through life with more peace and clarity. You stop punishing yourself for what someone else has done and start focusing on your own growth, healing, and well-being.

In the end, anger only hurts you, especially when it's tied to trying to control the uncontrollable. By letting go, you reclaim your power, choosing calm over chaos and peace over punishment.

Don't be easily offended

At first glance, this quote may feel harsh, but when explored deeply, it reveals a profound truth about emotional maturity and intellectual resilience. The quote is not meant to diminish anyone, but rather to highlight the relationship between emotional sensitivity and the capacity to think critically, calmly, and objectively.

When we are easily offended, it often stems from reacting emotionally before fully understanding or processing a situation. In these moments, our minds become clouded with hurt, anger, or frustration, making it difficult to engage with the issue thoughtfully. This is not about intelligence in terms of IQ, but about intellectual maturity, the ability to step back, assess, and approach a situation with calmness rather than instant reaction. So, when someone is quick to take offense, they are less likely to think rationally, listen deeply, or consider different perspectives.

Ask yourself: What happens when you feel offended? Do you jump to conclusions, take things personally, or let your emotions guide your response? In these moments, you may feel attacked or misunderstood, but is that truly what is happening? Or could it be that you're allowing your emotions to override a more thoughtful, considered approach? When we allow ourselves to be easily offended, we limit our ability to engage in meaningful conversations and to see situations from multiple angles.

Imagine a scenario where someone says something you don't agree with or criticizes you in a way that feels personal. If your first reaction is to take offense, you shut down the possibility of learning or understanding. Instead of asking questions, seeking clarity, or considering their perspective, you put up a mental wall. This defensive stance makes it hard to reflect on whether there is any truth in the other person's words or whether you can gain new insights from the situation. By reacting this way, you miss out on opportunities for growth, self-reflection, and improvement.

Now, think about the opposite: What happens when you choose not to be offended so easily? When you approach situations with curiosity rather than defensiveness, you create space for deeper understanding. You become more resilient, more willing to hear different opinions, and more open to constructive criticism. This intellectual openness enhances your ability to think critically, ask thoughtful questions, and engage in more meaningful discussions.

Being less easily offended is not about suppressing your emotions or ignoring disrespect. It's about having the emotional intelligence to assess situations calmly, knowing when to respond and when to let go. It's about recognizing that not every remark is an attack, and not every disagreement is a personal insult. The more we can separate our emotions from our thinking, the more intelligently we can navigate conversations and conflicts.

The quote invites you to ask yourself: Do I want to react emotionally and shut down my ability to learn and grow? Or do I want to cultivate resilience, patience, and deeper understanding? Intelligence in this context is not just about being smart, it's about being able to rise above immediate reactions and approach life's challenges with an open, thoughtful mind.

The less easily you are offended, the more you engage with life from a place of wisdom rather than reaction, and in doing so, you allow yourself to grow intellectually, emotionally, and personally.

Chapter 39

God is in control

You relax on a bus without knowing the driver. You relax on a plane without knowing the pilot. Every day, without even realizing it, you place your trust in processes beyond your control. This simple act of faith, trusting in the expertise of others, in systems that work, is what allows you to move through life with less stress and more ease. You trust that the bus will take you to your destination, or that the plane will land safely, and in doing so, you free yourself from worrying about every detail.

The same principle applies to your own life. Placing faith in the process allows you to shift your energy from worrying about things outside your control to focusing on what you can do. When you learn to let go of the need to control everything, you gain peace of mind and the ability to channel your efforts toward what truly matters. Life is full of uncertainties, and while it's natural to want control, constantly trying to manage the unknown only leads to stress and anxiety.

Imagine if, instead of stressing over the mechanics of every situation, you allowed yourself to trust the process, just as you trust the driver or pilot. This doesn't mean sitting back and doing nothing it means focusing your energy on the things you can influence while letting go of the rest. You control your actions, your mindset, and how you respond to challenges. The rest the outcomes, the timing, the unforeseen events are beyond your reach.

By placing your faith in the process, you give yourself permission to focus on your growth, your actions, and your choices. You free up mental and emotional space to concentrate on what's important, rather than wasting energy on things that are out of your hands. When you trust that life will unfold as it's meant to, just like the bus will reach its destination, you release the need for constant control.

This doesn't mean that life will always go according to plan or that there won't be bumps along the way. But by trusting the process, you understand that not everything is your responsibility to manage. There will always be forces at work beyond your control, but your power lies in how you navigate through those moments. Trusting the process helps you maintain a sense of calm, knowing that you are doing your part while allowing life to unfold naturally.

So, just as you relax on a journey without knowing the driver or the pilot, allow yourself to relax in your own life. Focus on what you can control: your mindset, your actions, your choices. Trust that the process will carry you where you need to go, and in doing so, you'll find more peace, focus, and strength.

Stop worrying

Worrying is like worshipping the problem. When you worry, you are giving your energy, focus, and attention to the issue at hand, almost as if you are elevating it to a place of importance in your mind. The more you worry, the more power the problem holds over you, consuming your thoughts and dictating your emotions. In this way, worrying doesn't solve the problem, it amplifies it.

Worry often stems from fear of the unknown or an inability to control a situation. It's natural to feel anxious about things we care about or want to resolve, but when we let worry take over, we become fixated on the problem itself rather than on finding a solution. It's like constantly thinking about a fire but never reaching for the water to put it out. We focus so much on the worst possible outcomes that we fail to consider how to move forward or how to manage the situation constructively.

When you worry, you are essentially devoting time and mental energy to the problem, almost like worshipping it. Just as worship involves dedication, focus, and belief, worrying involves giving your full attention to what could go wrong. You end up trapped in a cycle of fear and anxiety, repeatedly thinking about potential negative outcomes rather than looking for a way to resolve or accept the situation. Worry becomes the center of your thoughts, and soon, it becomes difficult to see anything else.

But here's the thing: worrying doesn't change the situation. No amount of worrying has ever solved a problem or made things better. Instead, it keeps you stuck, draining your energy and leaving you feeling powerless. You're so busy worrying that you miss the opportunity to take action, or you overlook the possibility of positive outcomes. It's like focusing on the shadow rather than the light, unable to see a way out.

The truth is, you can't always control what happens, but you can control how you respond to it. Instead of worrying, ask yourself,

"What can I do right now to improve this situation?" or "What is within my control?" Shifting your focus from the problem to potential solutions not only empowers you, but it also gives you back the energy you were spending on worry. Even if the situation is beyond your control, you can choose to focus on acceptance and finding peace with whatever outcome unfolds.

It's important to recognize that worrying creates a false sense of productivity. We often feel like we're doing something by worrying about an issue, but in reality, we're just feeding the problem with our attention. When we break the habit of worrying, we free ourselves to think more clearly and act more decisively. We move from a place of fear to a place of empowerment.

So, the next time you find yourself worrying, remind yourself that worry is like worshipping the problem. Instead of giving it power, direct your energy toward solutions, mindfulness, or acceptance. By shifting your focus, you break the cycle of worry and allow yourself to move forward. Remember, worrying doesn't change the outcome, but how you choose to respond to the situation does.

Stop doubting yourself

Far too often, we hold ourselves back, not because we lack the ability, but because we let doubt cloud our vision. That little voice in our heads telling us we're not good enough, not capable, or not ready can be louder than anything else. But here's the truth: the only thing stopping you from achieving what you want is you.

You have the capacity to succeed. Whether it's reaching a personal goal, starting a new project, or making a major life change, you already possess the skills, strength, and resilience needed to get there. The problem isn't your lack of talent or opportunity; it's the way you limit yourself with self-doubt. Every time you question your ability, you're putting up an imaginary barrier between yourself and what you want.

We often allow fear to take control fear of failure, of rejection, or of the unknown. But fear is not a signal that you're incapable. It's a natural response to stepping outside of your comfort zone. Every challenge you face is an opportunity to grow, to learn, and to prove to yourself that you are stronger than your doubts. When you let fear dictate your actions, you remain stuck in place, never discovering what you're truly capable of.

The most important thing to understand is that you have control over who you are and what you become. Every day, with every choice, you're shaping your future. The decisions you make, the risks you take, and the actions you commit to are all within your power. By continuing to doubt yourself, you're handing that power over to fear and uncertainty. But when you choose to believe in yourself, to trust in your abilities, you take control of your life and open the door to success.

You are not defined by your past failures or by the limitations others place on you. The only real limitations are the ones you create for yourself. The people who achieve great things aren't necessarily the smartest, most talented, or luckiest, they're the ones who kept pushing forward despite their doubts. They decided to believe in their potential and took action even when the outcome wasn't guaranteed.

You have the power to do the same. Stop waiting for the "perfect" time or the "perfect" plan. The perfect moment to start will never come because growth happens through action, not through waiting. Start with what you have, where you are, and trust that as you take steps forward, you'll figure out the rest along the way.

It's time to stop doubting your potential. You are capable of more than you know, and the only thing holding you back is your belief that you can't. But the truth is, you can. You've got everything you need inside of you to succeed. All you have to do is trust in yourself, push past your doubts, and take control of your own path.

Chapter 40

Break free from expectations

There will come a time in life when people will regret the way they treated you. Not because you sought their validation, but because you outgrew the expectations and assumptions they placed on you. Often, others treat us based on how they perceive us, boxed into roles that fit their narrative, limited by their own insecurities or misguided judgments. They assume you'll stay the same, never change, and continue accepting the treatment you've always received. But when you begin to fully focus on yourself, on your growth, and on your worth, everything changes. And that's when their regret begins to surface.

For so long, you may have been influenced by what others thought of you. Maybe you tried to meet their expectations or allowed their opinions to shape your self-image. It's easy to get caught up in valuing other people's views of us more than our own. We often allow their words, their judgments, and even their indifference to dictate our sense of worth. But here's the truth: you are far more than what anyone else thinks of you. The moment you understand this, deeply and truly, is the moment you reclaim your power.

When you focus inward, tuning out the noise of what others expect or assume, you start to see yourself in a whole new light. You realize that their opinions, no matter how strong or how hurtful, do not define you. You begin to rise above the limitations they placed on you, breaking free of the boxes they tried to keep you in. And it's not done out of spite or the desire for revenge, it's done out of a genuine love and respect for yourself.

The moment you shift your focus from seeking validation to cultivating your own self-esteem, something remarkable happens. You become unshakable. Your energy shifts. The things that used to hurt or diminish you lose their power. You begin to grow into the person you were always meant to be, someone who is confident, empowered, and self-assured. And it's in that moment, when you fully step into your own worth, that those who once underestimated you start to see the truth.

Regret often follows when people realize they didn't see your potential, that they took your kindness for weakness or your silence for acceptance. They regret treating you wrong because they come to understand that they never truly knew you, or worse, they took you for granted. As you elevate yourself, breaking free from the opinions and limitations of others, they are left to confront their own choices, the times they underestimated you, disrespected you, or didn't value what you had to offer.

But this journey isn't about making them regret their actions. It's about you learning to place your self-esteem and worth above all else. It's about recognizing that the opinions of others, whether positive or negative should never dictate your path or your sense of value. Their regret is a by-product of your growth, not the goal. The true reward is in the freedom and strength you gain by living authentically and unapologetically for yourself.

People will regret how they treated you when they realize you've become everything they never expected you to be. But by that point, it won't matter to you anymore, because you will have already outgrown the need for their approval. You will be too focused on the richness of your own journey, the fulfilment that comes from valuing yourself above all else.

So, let them have their regret. You have something far more valuable, your self-respect, your self-worth, and the clarity that comes from knowing your value is not determined by how others see you, but by how you see yourself. Keep focusing on yourself, keep growing, and know that breaking free from the expectations of others is one of the greatest forms of empowerment. You are already enough, just as you are.

Enjoy the moment

Take a moment and ask yourself: what do you truly want to do before you die? Strip away the distractions, the pressures of everyday life, and the noise of other people's expectations. What are the things that matter most to you, the dreams you've tucked away, the experiences you long for, the things that set your soul on fire?

Too often, we live as though tomorrow is guaranteed. We push our desires, our passions, and our dreams into a future that might never come. We get caught up in routines, postponing the things that truly matter in the hope that "one day" we'll get to them. But what if that "one day" is now? What if today is the only guarantee you have?

This moment is an opportunity to go on an inner journey. It's not about what society expects of you, or what you think you "should" want. It's about digging deep and finding what you "truly" want out of life. What experiences would make your life feel complete? What goals would give you a sense of fulfilment? What memories do you want to create, and who do you want to share them with?

Is there a place you've always wanted to visit, a skill you've always wanted to master, or a conversation you've been too afraid to have? Have you been holding back from telling someone how much they mean to you, or from taking a leap of faith in your career, relationships, or personal life? These desires live inside of you for a reason, they are a part of your purpose, and a part of what will make your journey through life uniquely yours.

Now, imagine living every day as if it were your last. Not in fear, but in gratitude. Waking up each morning with the knowledge that today is a gift, an opportunity to move closer to the things you love, the people who matter, and the experiences that will bring you joy. When you live this way, the small worries and fears that hold you back begin to fade. You start to see life with more clarity, realizing that time is your most precious resource and that every day, every moment, is a chance to live fully.

What would you change if you knew there was no time to waste? What would you prioritize if you knew you had only today to make an impact? This isn't about rushing or overwhelming yourself; it's about aligning with what matters most. It's about making sure that, when you look back on your life, you do so with a deep sense of satisfaction, knowing that you lived it on your own terms.

Let today be the day you start living more intentionally. Take the time to reflect on what truly drives you, what ignites your passion, and what fills your heart with joy. Then, take one step toward that vision, no matter how small it may seem. Life doesn't have to be perfect to be meaningful, but it does have to be authentic to you.

Don't wait for "someday" to start living the life you want. That day may never come. Instead, start now. Honour the dreams that live inside you. Take risks, be bold, and chase the experiences that matter to you. Because when your time comes, you won't remember the things you didn't dare to do, you'll remember the things you embraced with all your heart. Live every day like it's your last, and you'll find that life becomes not just a series of moments, but a journey of meaning, passion, and fulfilment.

Love yourself

Love yourself, instead of loving the idea of other people loving you. Take a moment to ask yourself: where do you seek love? Is it from within, or are you constantly looking for it in the approval, validation, or affection of others? It's easy to get caught up in wanting to be loved by others, but have you ever wondered why? What is it that makes their love seem more valuable than your own?

Do you find yourself changing or hiding parts of who you are just to feel accepted? Do you crave the attention of others to feel worthy or complete? These are important questions because they point to a deeper truth, when we prioritize the love of others over self-love, we give away our power. We begin to rely on external validation to feel good about ourselves, forgetting that the most important source of love must come from within.

Have you ever asked yourself: Why do I struggle to love myself as I am? What is it that makes me think someone else's approval holds more value than my own? Do I truly see my worth, or am I waiting for someone else to validate it?

The more you seek love from others without first giving it to yourself, the more you create a gap inside, a space where self-doubt and insecurity grow. You start living for how others perceive you, forgetting that no amount of external love can fill a void that can only be filled by your own acceptance. Loving the idea of others loving you might give you temporary satisfaction, but it will never lead to true fulfilment.

Ask yourself this: What would change if I focused on loving myself, truly, deeply, and without conditions? What parts of me have I been neglecting because I've been too focused on seeking love from outside sources? Am I waiting for someone else to show me my worth when, in reality, I could already see it for myself?

When you start to love yourself, something beautiful happens. You stop needing others' approval to feel complete. You stop chasing love because you realize you already have it. You begin to feel at peace with who you are, flaws and all, and that kind of self-love is the foundation for everything else. It's not about being perfect; it's about being real, authentic, and compassionate toward yourself.

So, why wait for others to give you what you can already give yourself? Why base your worth on someone else's feelings or perceptions when you have the power to define it yourself? When you love yourself, the need for others to fill that space fades, and instead, you find that the love you receive from others becomes a reflection of the love you've already given to yourself.

Take the time to reflect on these questions. Shift your focus inward and realize that the love you've been seeking from others has always been within your reach. Once you embrace that, you'll not only attract more genuine love into your life, but you'll also live with the freedom and confidence that comes from knowing you are enough, just as you are.

End

About the Author

Lame Lesego Rakgantswana

Lame Lesego Rakgantswana is an expert in business, accounting, finance and taxation. She studied business and gained experience providing accounting, finance and taxation services to clients. She published books titled *Value Within: 16 solution oriented Approaches to self worth* and *Confident: Developing exceptional self-confidence.*